COMPANY INK

SAMANTHA ANNE

Copyright © 2015 Samantha Molina

All rights reserved.

This book, or parts thereof, may not be reproduced in any form without permission from the publisher; exceptions are made for brief excerpts used in published reviews.

Published by:

Cookies & Queens Publishing

Arlington, TX 76010, USA

www.samantha-anne.net

ISBN: 9781796669909

This is a work of fiction. Names, characters, corporations, institutions, organizations, events, or locales in this novel are either the product of the author's imagination. The resemblance of any character to actual persons (living or dead) is entirely coincidental.

Cover art: freepik.com/Samantha Anne

Dedication

"Love is lovelier, the second time around..."

This 2nd Edition remains dedicated to all the romance readers who like a little spice with their sugar. May all your endings be happy, in every sense of the word!

Acknowledgments

Thanks to Julie for helping me get more juice from these pages – I couldn't stand for this book to be off the market, and your editorial help is a huge reason why!

Sending all of my love to the family and friends that have been my biggest fans from the beginning – thank you for your reviews, social media shares, and all the books of mine you've given to others as gifts!

Remember to always be your most authentic self, whether that truth is kinky, vanilla, or (in the case of Ben & Violet in the pages ahead) somewhere in between - I love you always.

Chapter One

*B*en Preston stepped into Wynne's Kitchen at Rockefeller Center, knowing full well these next few minutes would determine whether he would take over this store or not. The only information the H.R. manager had divulged was that the last general manager had emotionally collapsed under the weight of the numbers the popular dessert bakery saw on a daily basis, so they were looking for a GM who could handle volume, particularly in a fast-paced environment.

Fast-paced was practically Ben's middle name. And even though he had admitted his complete lack of bakery experience, the H.R. manager insisted he meet with Wynne and take a look around their Rockefeller Center location. It wasn't overconfidence that kept him from being surprised, because he worked hard for his reputation—he was the captain, the go-to guy when a company needed a location to succeed.

Ben waded his way through the crowd that waited for service while the counter staff grabbed and bagged items as fast as they could, managing to do so with smiles on their faces. All this for cupcakes and pastries? At least this place could provide the much-needed distraction from his pending divorce.

Spotting the woman he guessed to be his new boss, Wynne Lansing, he made his way toward the register. She was all sophistication, even in an apron and street clothes, with a bandana tied around her auburn hair. She looked as if she was ready to throw down in the kitchen with the rest of the bakers. Wynne must have wanted to illustrate that she still remained active in day-to-day operations. Chuckling inwardly, Ben smiled and took her hand to shake it as he introduced himself.

"Wow," Wynne remarked as she leaned back to get a better look at him. "How tall are you?"

"Six-four, ma'am," he answered with a smile. "I come from a family of Vikings." "Clearly! Well, we have some low ceilings in the basement, so be careful."

"I'll be sure to do that. So, tell me about this place."

Wynne nodded, motioning for him to follow her down into the basement. Her voice was loud and clear over the roar of the excited customers shouting their orders. "This is our flagship location. We call it The Rock for two reasons. One—obviously—we're at Rockefeller Center. Two, this location consistently sells the most product, sees the most traffic, and is the highest-rated unit in the entire company. We need someone here who won't just maintain its status but will strive to make it better."

"Gotcha," he replied, narrowly avoiding slamming his head on a low ceiling. "How are the other stores performing?"

Wynne practically dashed through what Ben immediately knew to be the prep area. "They're all doing great, given their locations and challenges. We were hoping to see how you do here, then potentially have you move through the other locations to see what kind of magic you work there."

He'd already spotted areas throughout the store where his strict fine-dining background might be completely useless. But he also saw where his expertise could be injected, so the fact that Wynne seemed to have already pegged him as the guy to get the job done was encouraging. He'd spent a lot of time in recent weeks questioning everything about his career and life in general—so the ego stroke was rather validating.

"So are you saying I have the job?"

Wynne stopped and turned around. "You came highly recommended. Everyone we called had nothing but amazing things to say about you. I want you with Wynne's Kitchen. And I'm prepared to meet your salary requirements and exceed them when you prove that your incredible reputation is not unwarranted."

Ben chuckled. "This is all very intense."

Wynne shrugged with a grin. "I know what I want."

"I see that," Ben replied. "I'm happy to come on board and, frankly, thankful that you've put so much faith in me."

"It's my pleasure," Wynne said. "I recently hired a production supervisor in your same position. She lacked experience but has all of the skills I'm looking for to do great. And so do you. We're a great team, and I know you'll get the support you need to excel, just like she did. So, do I need to give you a tour of the prep area?"

"Actually, it's pretty compact. I'm guessing I could point out the sections without doing much more than a spin: prep, dry storage, walk-in, paper goods."

Wynne laughed. "Exactly. Let's show you around upstairs, and we'll get your paperwork started."

They breezed back through the prep area, where he

couldn't help but notice the amazing smell of caramel as a cook whisked vigorously in a metal saucepan. Ben led the way up the stairs, gradually becoming more excited about the new job with every step he took. He turned the corner to the hallway that led to the main floor and was suddenly met with a pair of eyes that looked like two pools of silvery silk.

He stopped short, his sneakers squeaking as he did so. Ben's vision focused on an unknown woman staring back at him, looking about as surprised as he did that they'd managed to avoid colliding. She was tall, and her jet-black hair was bundled up in a hair net. She clutched her clipboard and continued to stare at him fixedly, her eyes wide. His eyes involuntarily scanned her body. Built like the sexiest of female superheroes, her solid body curved more dangerously than a winding road. He forced his eyes to focus on her forehead. *So unprofessional.*

Wynne stepped around Ben, breaking the trance between him and the girl. "Oh, good—just in time! This young lady is your production supervisor. You'll be working closely together; she handles all of the production and makes sure you don't waste money on unused product. She'll be your greatest asset while you're getting to know this store. Ben, meet Violet."

He took a deep breath as he nodded in greeting, knowing full well that with Violet in his store, he was in for a challenge bigger than he ever could have anticipated.

∼

VIOLET TRAILED behind Ben and Wynne as they headed toward the cake icer's station. She wasn't sure what she'd given away when their eyes met, but she was sure she'd felt her face go from zero to fiery in less than a couple of seconds. She hadn't reacted that way toward a guy since she'd come to her senses three years ago and left Mr. All Wrong. As a result, she had grown used to being a cool-headed, naturally flirtatious, next-door- neighbor kind of gal. The whole deer-in-headlights display wasn't a good look for her.

Life had led Violet to Wynne's Kitchen, and landing this job was a culmination of all the time she'd spent repairing and finding herself. While she didn't officially have the experience to qualify for the role of production supervisor, the years spent at her grandmother's knee combined with her time in culinary school provided her with the confidence she needed to be sure that she was the person Wynne needed for The Rock. That Wynne chose to take a chance on her meant Violet was one step closer to her ultimate dream: to own a cupcake shop of her own. But the addition of a new general manager left her more than a little wary.

She'd already gotten a bit of backstory about the new guy from Wynne less than an hour before his arrival. He had no bakery experience, but he'd once been a superstar in the world of fine dining. He was coming to Wynne's bakery after what Violet understood was a lengthy absence in the industry. Sure, he could probably turn over hundreds of tables a night and wow the elite with his knowledge of white linen service, but did he even know the difference between French and Swiss buttercream? Violet would never question Wynne's judgment, but, knowing what she knew about his résumé, she found herself decidedly unimpressed.

She stopped in the middle of the beverage section and examined Ben as closely as she could now that there was a bit of distance between them. He was tall—so tall. She imagined he had a build slightly larger than that of a swimmer, based on how the blue button-down shirt he wore clung to his shoulders. Her eyes wandered straight down the center of his chest, and she couldn't help but catch the casual way his slacks hung from his hips. His hair was dark blond, almost seeming brunette in some spots—slightly mussed, it gave him a devil-may-care appearance that forced one corner of Violet's mouth upward in a grin.

Violet couldn't miss the blue of his eyes, even from fifty feet away. And though his eyes were deep-set and authoritative, she spotted a kindness in them that would surely take her breath away if she stared for too long. Ben was, at first glance, remarkable. The thought of crushing again after such a long period of self-inflicted solitude made her smile from the inside out, but, given what she had at stake, she knew it was a horrible idea.

Ben wasn't just an obstacle on the way up the corporate ladder, he was a rung. One wrong move with him could jeopardize everything. The fact that he ignited a fire in the pit of her tummy that she hadn't felt in years was irrelevant. What mattered was whether the new guy's appearance in the bakery was going to be a blessing or a curse. And as she watched the muscles in his back flex beneath his shirt, she couldn't decide which it would be.

She watched with uncertainty as he schmoozed. Violet couldn't hear a word of what he was saying, but she knew immediately that Ben was just that guy. He obviously had the type of personality that attracted people to him. Having completed her first month at The Rock, she already knew Wynne wasn't an easy woman to impress. Yet there she was, hanging on to his every word. Violet raised an eyebrow as she studied him, a feeling of dread hitting her in the gut. Violet couldn't shake the feeling that helping with his training, as she promised Wynne, would be setting Ben up to climb right over her in the race for success.

Ben looked up as if he finally felt her eyes on him. In her rush to feign disinterest, she dropped her clipboard. It bounced off the ergonomic mats and hit the cabinet door beneath the back counter, with a loud clatter. To her horror, everyone behind the counter stopped to look at her; beet-red, she ran her hands down her face. Grumbling, she picked up her clipboard and made a beeline for her station, where Ben and Wynne were waiting.

"Here's our girl." Her boss beamed. "Violet, show Ben how you ice a nine-inch, three-layer cake in less than four minutes."

Ben gave Violet an interested smile. "Less than four minutes?"

"Care to time me?" She pulled a stopwatch from beneath the counter. While part of her couldn't wait to show off, another part of her prayed she wouldn't stare the hot general manager in the face and drop the cake.

He took the stopwatch from Violet and glanced toward Wynne. "She's confident, I'll give her that."

Wynne nodded with a proud smile. "Watch her."

"Go ahead, Ben," Violet pressed with a smile that may have been more flirtatious than she intended. "Start the clock."

"Don't you want to set up first?"

She shook her head but stood close to the cooling rack with her hands reaching for the a large metal sheet pan, on which sat three vanilla cake layers. He regarded her with a mischievous grin as he clicked the stopwatch. Without a word, she slipped on a pair of food-safe, latex gloves and went to work, her motions fluid and quick as she grabbed the sheet pan that held all the cooled cake layers and placed it on the counter in front of her. She then grabbed a decorating turntable, a bucket of chocolate buttercream, and a fresh icing wand. On top of the turntable, she placed a cardboard cake round, then a doily, and then a dollop of icing followed by a cake layer. The turntable spun beneath her expert hands as she continued.

Icing, cake layer, icing—she felt eyes on her from all around, but it didn't sway her concentration. She swirled, smoothed, and swiped until her cake was a delicious tower of vanilla and chocolate flavors. With a final flourish, she looked up. People watching from the display window smiled, nodding and gesturing their admiration from outside. She looked to Ben, who gave her an impressed grin as he stopped the stopwatch.

"Three minutes," he remarked, although she suspected he was trying hard to avoid sounding too enthusiastic. "That's amazing. And it looks beautiful. How long did it take for you to learn that?"

"The technique? Not long. But I've been baking and decorating for pretty much my whole life, so this all comes naturally to me."

Wynne patted Violet's shoulder affectionately. "I have to get down to the office to check in on that paperwork. Why don't you and Ben spend a little time together? You can show him the ropes."

Violet stripped off her gloves and placed her hands on the counter, dropping her head as she stifled a giggle. Rope-showing techniques definitely came to mind, though none of them had anything to do with decorating cakes. Brushing those thoughts aside, she simply nodded in response and grabbed another set of cake layers that had finished cooling and were ready for icing.

When she faced Ben, she noticed he was examining the cake closely. Taking a deep breath to steel herself, she ended up being rewarded with a dizzying whiff of his cologne. The smell of Encounter by Calvin Klein filled her nostrils, and her eyes closed involuntarily. He remained in position as he looked over the cake and muttered compliments, totally unaware of the effect he was having on her. And when his arms brushed against her, butterflies rose in her tummy as pure electricity passed between them. His body went rigid, and he leaned in ever so slightly.

He must have felt it too. Her breath caught in her throat, and she thought she heard Ben inhale.

"You smell like cupcakes," he said, looking down at her with a spark of lust in his eyes.

Her lips parted, but she couldn't speak. Violet became very aware of the fact that he was watching her mouth. *Am I wearing gloss today?* she wondered wildly as they remained frozen in place. Out of the corner of her eye, she spotted a couple of onlookers watching through the window with both delighted and scandalized expressions. Forcing herself back to reality, she cleared her throat and focused on the cake she'd just iced.

"Yeah, well," she answered, "like I said, I've been baking forever. I guess my skin eventually absorbed a little batter."

Ben forced a laugh, and Violet followed suit to lighten the mood, all the while silently begging for someone, anyone, to come over and get involved in the conversation. How the hell was she supposed to train this human tower of sexy without getting distracted by his crystal-blue eyes and the fact that he looked absolutely edible in casual dress?

"Maybe we should start with cupcakes," she continued. "They're just over here …"

She pivoted to the left at the exact same time he pivoted to the right; an awkward moment of silence extended between them as they were caught standing kissably close for the second time in less than five minutes. Violet thought herself a tall girl at five-foot-nine and a half; Ben towered over her in a way that she'd never quite been exposed to before, and it was unnerving.

Refusing to meet his eyes, she ended up staring at his chest. Her heart thumped madly; she hadn't realized he'd removed his tie. A button had come undone, revealing a sprinkling of hair and a peek at his strong chest. She glanced upward through her eyelashes and realized that not only were Ben's eyes on her again, but he looked as flustered as she was.

I have no time in my life to get distracted by you, Ben Preston, she sighed inwardly. *This guy can't be the reason I let myself down.*

She took a step back. "How about you grab an apron from downstairs? Make sure you put on a hat or a hairnet."

"Yeah, good idea. I'll be right back, Violet."

She gripped the counter for dear life as her knees went weak at the sound of his voice practically crooning her name. Day one with the new general manager was already proving to be a disaster—she'd known Ben less than an hour and already wanted to slather him in buttercream. She pressed her hand against her forehead, only to groan when she realized that not only did she slap a small glob of icing onto her face, but she'd also need to change gloves again.

~

BEN CAME home to an empty apartment and his landline ringing off the hook. He dropped his jacket on the floor

Company Ink

and strode to the corner of the floor where his phone sat. He checked the caller ID, then scoffed as he picked up.

"You know I have a cell phone, right?"

"I tried your cell phone earlier; it kept going straight to voicemail," a young female said. "Mom was afraid you committed suicide."

Ben sighed, pressing his back against the wall and sliding down to sit. "I'm sure Elena would like that. We're still technically married, so she'd get everything."

"Seriously, bro. How are you?"

He smiled to himself as he imagined his sister, Lisa, sitting cross-legged on his mother's couch with a worried look on her face. She was nearly ten years younger but very protective of him and, in many ways, one of his closest friends despite their age difference.

"Really, Lis, I'm fine. And how are you? Still living at home, I see," he teased.

"Hey, back off. I'm in college and working. Mom's not getting rid of me until I've got my master's."

He chuckled. "I don't think you're at any risk of Mom throwing you out anyway. You're the best cook in the house."

"How about you? It's been weeks. Are you moving back home or what?"

"I'm staying here in the city. I decided I'm not going to let Elena run me out of here. This is my place, my money paid for it."

Lisa was silent for a moment. "Ben, she came by today."

The news startled him; he pushed off the wall and sat straight up. "She went to the house? What the hell for?"

"She came over to say goodbye apparently, or that's what she wanted us to believe. She had tears in her eyes, parting gifts, and everything."

"Well, she's got the award for best actress in the bag."

"She definitely does. But," Lisa paused again, "that wasn't all she said."

He let out a sigh. "I'm not gonna like this. All right, what did she say?"

"Promise me you won't get mad. You don't need any more stress …"

"Lis, there's no way that anything involving Elena isn't going to piss me off, okay? So just spit it out."

"Fine, fine. She was also telling us that you're mentally disturbed and you'd been emotionally abusive the entire time you two were together."

Speechless, Ben felt his blood begin to boil immediately. All those times he'd come home with flowers and woke up the next day to find them in the garbage. After a while, Elena never let him touch her and often coordinated her returns home with times she knew he'd be asleep. All the lies, all the tricks—what it came down to, ultimately, was that Elena played him for a fool. His head began to throb; he pinched the bridge of his nose between his thumb and forefinger.

"Ben?"

"What did Mom say? Why did you actually call me?"

"I called to make sure you were okay, I swear!"

He could feel the bile rising in his throat. "Do you actually believe her?"

"No, I know she's lying," Lisa insisted, "but Mom sort of ate it up. Elena told her that you threatened to kill yourself if she didn't come back."

"Shit, are you serious?"

"I managed to calm Mom down after she left, but she's worried about you. She's afraid you're gonna hurt either yourself or Elena."

Company Ink

Ben's head dropped as he clutched the phone tightly. "I can't deal with this right now."

"Bro, I know she's lying. And I'm sure Mom knows, deep down, that Elena's full of crap. But you gotta be careful. I don't know, but I think that piece of trash is out for blood."

"I just wanna get on with my life."

His statement was met with silence; he knew his sister didn't know what to say. Then again, he didn't expect her to. No one expected this bomb his soon-to-be ex had dropped on him, not even Lisa, who, from day one, always seemed a little put out by his ex-wife's presence. And Elena's proverbial kick to the groin had been more than he was prepared to deal with, at least for tonight. Suddenly, the news of a new job and an unexpected spark of attraction with someone seemed like nonsense.

"Look, I've gotta go," he said. "But you should come out and spend some time with me. Give me a couple of weeks to furnish my place again, and you'll see I'm fine."

"I know you're fine. But okay. I'll talk to you later?"

"Yeah, good night."

He hung up the phone and trudged toward the master bedroom, where a raised air mattress sat waiting for him. He stopped at the fridge for the last beer before finally calling it a night. In the bare walls of his bedroom, he kicked off his shoes and pushed them against the far wall, where the dresser once stood. Placing the beer bottle on the floor next to the mattress, he pulled his shirt off and hung it on one of the ten hangers Elena had left in the closet. The emptiness of the room contributed to the lousy feeling that radiated through his body, but tomorrow would be a new day. Sleep might take hours at this point, but the beer would at least help get Elena out of his head.

SAMANTHA ANNE

∼

VIOLET SAT sideways on the couch next to her best friend, Ella. It was a rare weekend; they were finally taking a Saturday to stay home in their pajamas with a bottle of wine and a couple of John Hughes flicks.

"So tell me all about this new general manager! Where did he come from?"

Violet ran her hands down her face with a flustered giggle. "Damned if I know! But he's so much yum, I can't stand it."

"It's been way too long. Steve almost broke you, girl."

Violet let out a sigh of agreement. From ages fourteen to eighteen, Violet had been absolutely smitten with the adorable football player. Even as a teenager, he had a type of definition to his body that would have made men twice his age jealous. They had always been friends but, despite how much she liked him, she was never able to build up the courage to tell him. And though she landed her first boyfriend at sixteen, she'd still crushed. High school ended, her relationship ended, and she never stopped dreaming about Quarterback Steve.

But their paths hadn't crossed again until Violet was wrapping up an associate's degree in business management and looking for a new adventure. On a whim, she signed up with her high school alumni association as part of her internship requirements. It was during an alumni mixer that she ran into Steve. He was pouring himself a Scotch and soda; she was working the hors d'oeuvre table.

He was starting a career with the coaching staff of the New York Jets at just twenty- one. And at twenty, she knew he was everything she wanted in a guy. But their love didn't last, and an unhealthy obsession made him hard to quit. The level of drama over the six years they were together left her heartbroken, nearly financially broken, and inexplicably damaged. And while she'd felt unable to trust or rely on the opposite sex, she knew the experience had left her stronger, even though she was technically still healing. That was when Violet decided to use the rest of her grandmother's money to do what she should have done from the beginning. She threw herself into culinary arts and restaurant management—and piles of pastry flour and batches of marzipan quite literally brought her back to life.

She looked to Ella with a smile. "I haven't actually crushed in a long time. It feels nice."

"You certainly were the crush queen." Ella laughed. "But it's nice to see you back. You're gonna go for it, right?"

"Are you out of your mind? He's my manager!"

"There's nothing wrong with dipping your pen in the company ink!"

Violet shook her head, standing up to pour herself another glass of wine. "No, sweetie, everything is wrong with dipping in the ... ugh, I don't even want to say it!"

"Come on, Vi! What harm can it do?"

Violet let out an exasperated sigh before saying, "Are you the devil or something? I'm busy trying to build my empire, and you want me to hit on management?"

"For starters," Ella replied with a wink. "From the sound of things there's a lot more heating up in that bakery than just the ovens! And besides, you only live once."

Violet grinned despite her best attempt at being dramatically shocked. "I can't take you sometimes. The worst thing I could possibly do is hit on Ben Preston." She carefully sat back on the couch, her wine glass lifted to her lips. "Sure, he's built like a demigod. And his tush looks amazing in khakis."

Ella nodded, polishing off her glass. "Mmm-hmm. Deny it to yourself if you want, chica, but you can't fool me."

Violet narrowed her eyes playfully as she glanced at her best friend. "I hate you."

"No, you love me, doll. And mark my words, Vi, this isn't over."

Chapter Two

Violet took brisk steps from the train to the bakery on Tuesday, after a couple of well-deserved days off. The bounce in her step could have easily been because of the gentle breeze in the air or the sound of the birds as they slowly awoke from their nightly slumber. She'd always been happy to go to work since starting at Wynne's Kitchen. From the beginning, Violet was given the freedom to test recipes and meet with Wynne at any point when an especially tasty idea came to mind, thanks to Wynne's genuine interest in her development as a baker. She reveled in making Wynne proud; the older, sophisticated woman shared many of Violet's grandmother's personality traits and, as a result, she and Wynne had already formed a special bond. She also loved spending hours decorating cakes, chatting up customers, and making their buttercream dreams come to life with a wave of her icing wand.

Life had gotten a little more complicated with Ben on the team, Violet knew, even having spent only one afternoon with him before her weekend started. They'd spent the bulk of his working interview at her station, chatting about production and going over the menu. She knew helping to introduce a new manager to the busiest bakery in the company would be trying and, quite frankly, a pain in the ass. After all, she had promised Wynne she'd give it her all when it came to getting the new guy acclimated to working at The Rock. But damn—the guy didn't seem to have a clue.

On a daily basis, Vi was responsible for fulfilling orders to be picked up in the late morning or early afternoon. She also made sure that the bakers and prep cooks were following their lists to the letter and had to deal directly with the general manager if any of the food inventory needed replenishing. And while Violet prided herself on being reliable as all get-out, the general manager needed to know her job inside and out ... obviously. He seemed a little stunned by all the information she'd offered up in a short period of time. His facial expression was enough to let her know that training this guy would be no easy feat.

So far, Ben was a nice enough guy, but he seemed perplexed by The Rock's popularity with tourists. The fact that he didn't get the draw of the tastiest treat in the city had chipped away at Violet's nerves until she wasn't sure she even wanted to help the guy. She'd somehow gotten it in her head that he wouldn't take the job seriously, and for her, that meant trouble. Violet didn't want to spend time in a store where her ideas and work would go unnoticed because one of the people she was supposed to shine for didn't get it. By the end of her shift, her tolerance for Ben had been at zero. As she left, she'd hoped her brain would clear during her days off and she'd be able to start fresh when she came back.

Violet arrived at The Rock at 5:30 a.m., roughly a half hour before her shift was scheduled to start. She was

Company Ink

enjoying a cup of instant oatmeal and a banana in the office and couldn't help watching for Ben to walk through the door. The whole thing was weird—part of her wondered how much of the menu he'd forgotten, another part wondered if his eyes were as blue as she remembered. Having gotten so used to being engrossed in her greatest passion—baking—she wasn't even sure how she could be attracted to a guy who didn't know the difference between a tart and a pie.

"Get it together, Vi," she spoke aloud, pulling her curls into a ponytail and shoving it all under a hairnet.

The clock now said 6:00 a.m. With a shake of her head, she made her way upstairs to set up her station for the day. The store would be opening in an hour, so the counter staff was helping the kitchen crew by pulling cupcakes out of the oven and onto racks for cooling. Meanwhile, the morning bakers were scooping freshly prepared muffin batter into pans in preparation for the morning rush. Violet took a deep breath, inhaling the heavenly scent. *What a way to work.*

The counter staff had been gracious enough to start a pot of coffee for the rest of the openers; Violet thanked them all as she grabbed a large cup before taking the last few steps to her station situated in the front window of the bakery. She was almost afraid to look at last night's production list; the night manager, Jamie, loved to pile her list high no matter how often Violet reminded her that, as production supervisor, she couldn't spend all day stuck at her station. Jamie seemed to think that because Violet could ice a three-minute cake, there was no reason she couldn't bang out ten cakes in a half hour on a daily basis and then do twelve more. It was Jamie's corporate-machine mentality that Violet was never able to get on board with, so it was with a roll of her eyes that she made a mental note to drop a couple of those specialty cakes on the afternoon icer's list.

Setting up her icing wands, tips, and other tools took another five minutes, and she moved on to turning out the layers so that they could finish cooling. Violet looked up at the clock over the register bank; Ben was officially fifteen minutes late.

She forced the thought of him out of her mind and went to the center counter to help cut bars and set them out for service. *Who cares if he's late?* She scooped up salted caramel brownies with a spatula and placed them on miniature paper doilies. She was stacking them on a doily-topped cake dish when she heard a scraping sound come from the bakery's side entrance. Violet looked up to see Ben letting himself in, presumably with keys given to him by Jay, the operations manager. She lowered her gaze quickly as she waited for the bells over the door to chime as it opened.

When Ben entered, his eyes were dark and distant. Brow partially furrowed, he practically stared right through her before looking away and heading directly to the office downstairs.

Violet blinked a couple of times, his strange arrival taking her by surprise. For someone who was such a social butterfly on his first day, the apparent chip on his shoulder was an unexpected change. It made Violet nervous about what to expect for the rest of the day. After all, as Wynne reminded her before she left, Violet would be a crucial part of Ben's assimilation into the company.

Jessica, the store's floor supervisor, approached her with an ecstatic smile. "Vi, have you seen the new guy? My mornings just got much, much better."

"Yeah, I started training him last week."

Violet zoned out as Jessica began to talk animatedly

Company Ink

about Ben. Staring blankly ahead of her as she attached piping tips to their designated pastry bags, she wondered just how closely Jessica had worked with Ben in the two days since he'd joined the team. As the production supervisor, Violet would be interacting with him frequently where it concerned the quality and amount of baked goods being sold, but Jessica would be Ben's direct link to the floor when he was up to his elbows in administrative work during the day and, therefore, would interact just as much with him as Violet would, sometimes even more so. Violet frowned as she was visited with a sinking feeling that left a rock- sized lump in her tummy.

Jealous much?

"And you'll be training him all this week, Miss Production Sup," Jessica finished, nudging Violet playfully. "Just when I thought I'd hate your job, in walks Thor with a snazzy haircut."

Yanking herself out of the brooding, Violet turned toward her co-worker with a smile. "I'm sorry, are you swooning over our general manager?"

"Stop pretending you aren't as excited about training this guy as I am about ogling him all day," Jessica teased.

"Would you set up your floor already?" Violet dismissed with a laugh. "I've gotta have a quick talk with the bakers about the lemon muffins. I'm pretty sure if we double the batch we'll still sell out."

"Triple it if you want; the customers are nuts about those things. I'll check in with you later."

As Jessica made her way toward the cash registers, Violet leaned against the marble counter and placed a hand on her forehead. The reality that she would indeed be working closely with him sunk in and hit her hard. No one in the store knew the menu and its elements like Violet, regardless of the fact that she'd only been there a number of weeks. The other employees saw working at the bakery as a paycheck; to Violet, it was art, a labor of love, an important step on the road to realizing the dream of owning a bakeshop. Working at Wynne's Kitchen meant everything to her, so she buried herself in the job, getting to know every nook and cranny and committing it all to memory.

She had a lot to prove, in a manner of speaking, if she was going to climb the ranks successfully. And whether or not Ben would be a roadblock or a stepping stone still remained to be seen. She did know, however, that Wynne was counting on her to make the store's transition from old general manager to new general manager as smooth as possible. Violet didn't want to let her down. All she could hope for at this point was for her dedication to help advance her career with Wynne's Kitchen instead of turning her into a bottom-rung worker who would serve as everyone else's leg up.

She headed toward the baking area, where stacks of fresh baked muffins, cookies, and scones awaited her inspection, and tried to decide whether she should approach Ben or wait for him to come upstairs. Violet stared blankly ahead in a daze as she pulled a blueberry scone apart in her hands.

"Hey," a baker called out. "Vi, where are you?"

Violet looked down at the mutilated treat in her hands. *Damn.*

"Just checking consistency," she muttered dismissively, a horrible attempt at a save as she held it up toward him. "Good job, Mike. Make another half round."

Before the baker could say more, she dumped the scone on a nearby paper plate and balanced it on her clipboard. With a dessert allowance of one treat a day, this violated confection would have to be it for her. She grabbed her coffee and decided to gather her thoughts in the office, knowing in the back of her mind that was exactly where Ben would be.

Her feet carried her down the back stairs and through the prep area. Past the dry and cold storages and a few feet from the employee bathrooms lay the back office, where she and the other managers sat to either handle administrative duties, have lunch, or take phone orders. It was a large space, wide open except for the five workstations that lined three of the four walls. Lining the fourth wall, alongside the door, were cabinets and counters that held their copier, retail merchandise, extra polo shirts emblazoned with the bakery logo, and other office supplies.

With her eyes on Ben, she attempted to step in quietly, only to trip on the corner of a counter. She let out a tiny squeak as she narrowly avoided dropping everything. She cursed herself silently as Ben turned and looked at her. He looked tired.

"Good morning," she said.

"Hey, Violet," he muttered, his voice lacking spirit but somehow still sounding just as cozy as a down blanket. "Aren't you the lark?"

Violet grinned, taking a seat and carefully setting her coffee and scone down in front of her. "I take it you're not a morning person."

"Not lately," he replied, his voice transparently bitter.

His response made her stop short, surprised at how easily two words could be so off-putting. She stared at him briefly, nonplussed, trying to decide whether or not she should be offended, as he went back to counting the register drawer in front of him. A painfully awkward moment of silence passed between them; finally, Ben let out a deep sigh.

"Look, before you think I'm some kind of jerk, I just

want to apologize. I had a really rough"—he paused, seeming to check himself before continuing—"commute this morning. It was just a nightmare, and I'm kind of trying to get past it so I can get through the rest of the day."

"Oh." If anyone understood the commute through Midtown, it was Violet. "No worries. The city's rough, I know."

At that moment, the office door opened. Jay, the company's operations manager, stepped in with a smile. A twenty-something Puerto Rican from Queens, he often looked like he'd just stepped off the cover of a magazine despite being dressed for the bakery in a tee shirt and jeans. He normally worked in Wynne's corporate office near Central Park South but would be sticking around The Rock, at Wynne's insistence, to help Ben with the finer points of operating the bakery. Placing his messenger bag at the assistant manager's station, he flashed a grin at Violet before looking to Ben. A wide, friendly grin stretched across Ben's face as he met Jay in the middle of the office. They shook hands, and the Ben she'd first met completely emerged. *Night and day*, she couldn't help but think.

"Hey, sorry I'm late." Jay beamed, far more of a morning person than she and Ben combined. "How are you, Vi?"

She gladly returned Jay's friendly welcome. "Peachy keen, jelly bean! Training Ben today?"

Jay nodded. "I'll be working with him until about noon. After that, he's all yours. Wynne wants him learning to do production by the end of the week."

"You might have your work cut out for you, Violet. I'm used to a smaller menu with way fewer variations." Ben grinned.

Company Ink

She raised an eyebrow. *Oh, now we're running for office?* "You'll get it in no time, I'm sure."

"I'll check in with you when Jay's done with me."

"Sounds good," she replied. "I'll make sure my morning orders are done so we can focus on training."

Turning back to her scone, she listened halfheartedly to Ben's spirited conversation with Jay. His mood had flipped 180 degrees in a matter of seconds, and she couldn't help but feel like her head was spinning. She supposed she shouldn't hold his ability to schmooze against him; then again, she couldn't help but wonder what had caused him to yank up such an emotional wall. Why was she even interested?

Do you wanna save him, Vi?

She let out an amused snort that she hadn't meant to release.

Jay and Ben fell silent, abruptly stopping their conversation to stare at Violet. A slightly embarrassed smile tugged at the corners of her mouth as she looked around.

"Sorry," she mumbled coyly, putting her coffee cup to her lips.

Ben smiled at her, a genuine expression that made her heart race. She could've sworn it actually lit up the room. She watched him for longer than she meant to; her cheeks felt white-hot, and she straightened her back in response to the schoolgirl giggle deep inside her that threatened to emerge. He playfully winked at her and turned away. Violet was beyond happy that he was the first to look away, because her insides had already turned to magma. Her knees went weak, and she peered up at the ceiling, quietly thanking God for the existence of office chairs.

She thought she might have felt Ben's eyes on her after she turned back to face her computer screen, but she couldn't tell whether the laser-beam heat on her back was real or if she was just losing her mind. She sipped her coffee slowly as she confirmed a couple of online orders. Only when she heard Jay's voice and was certain Ben had been effectively distracted did she trust herself to stand. She'd almost made it out of the office when Jay spoke.

"We'll be up in a few minutes to do the opening huddle," he said. "Do me a favor and pass the word to Jess?"

"Sure thing." *Damn it, did my voice just crack?*

"See ya up there, Vi." There was a teasing edge in Ben's voice.

She turned and stared him in the eye, impulsively taking his tone of voice as a challenge. "It's Violet. And I'll see you later."

Ben looked a little taken aback. And as Violet made her way upstairs, she couldn't help but feel like things were probably going to get a lot more uncomfortable before they got better. Still, tiny fireworks set off in her stomach again as she thought of the deep-set, crystal-blue eyes that threatened to see right through her; this guy was already more trouble than he was worth. It was with a feeling of both excitement and apprehension that she welcomed whatever was coming between her and Ben.

~

VIOLET WAS HEAVILY FOCUSED on icing a red velvet cake, surrounded by tourists pressed against the glass that separated her from the crowd of people in the store as well as outside of it. She juggled creating perfect rosettes with answering questions from the curious customers who hoped to learn decorating secrets without the benefit of too much hard work. *I should be charging a consultation fee.* But the truth was, she loved chatting with the customers while she worked her magic. She was mid-conversation with a traveling photographer when her name was called.

"Hey, Vi!"

She looked over the crowd of customers and spotted Jay. She gave an exuberant wave and smiled while the photographer tried to snap a secret photo of her work.

"I'll see you tomorrow afternoon," he called. "Ben will be up to you in about half an hour."

Violet nodded. "See you tomorrow."

Focusing her attention back on the photographer, she spun her cake turntable. The now fully gussied-up cake slowly showed itself off. "You have to contact corporate if you plan on using that photo anywhere."

"Caught me, huh?"

Violet grinned. "It's not a big deal; they're pretty cool about photos. Just handle it properly, okay?"

The photographer nodded. "You got it, doll. Thanks for the chat!"

The pretty blond about Violet's age moved on to the cupcake counter while a curious family of tourists stepped up to engage Violet. She'd already gotten so used to chatting while she decorated that, as the family questioned Violet about her favorite desserts, she managed to ice a six-inch carrot cake with sweet cream-cheese icing and inscribe it before the line moved forward and the family said their goodbyes. She had just eased the cake onto a stainless-steel display stand and covered it with a clear plastic lid when she heard her name called.

Violet placed the cake in the refrigerated display case and turned in the direction of the voice. Ben was headed directly for her, weaving his way through the counter staff as they darted around each other on their quests to get customers through the line and out the door. He looked overwhelmed and rightfully so—it wasn't easy on the floor, where an employee could see hundreds of customers in the span of an hour on any given day and potentially box ten times the amount of cupcakes, cookies, or bars. She folded her arms and leaned against the marble counter at her station, waiting for his approach.

The look on his face said he might have still been feeling sunny; she chewed her bottom lip as her body tensed in anticipation of his arrival. He gave her a charming grin, and Violet melted only a little as one corner of his mouth turned up just a bit higher than the other.

"You're early," she said, turning away and reaching for the red bucket beneath her station.

"I know. I figured we can talk a little bit about whatever it is you're supposed to be helping me with. Thanks for doing that, by the way."

She pulled the scrub brush from the red bucket filled with cleaning solution and began to clean her countertop. "I'm glad to help. How are you doing with memorizing the menu?"

Ben grabbed a roll of paper towels. "There's literally twice as many items as there are on a restaurant menu. I can tell you how I'm doing, but I think you already know."

Violet's breath caught in her throat as his long, muscular arm reached around from behind her to offer her the paper towels. There was the scent she hadn't smelled since she first met him but somehow already knew as "him." She took the roll, maybe a little more aggressively than she meant to, and stepped around him to stand in front of the cooling rack.

"Well, that's exactly what I'm here to help you with," she said. "The job is a lot more than the office, and there aren't sets of organized little tables to check on or turn over. It's a different beast."

Company Ink

"I hear you loud and clear. That's why I came up early. Where should we start?"

Violet laid a hand on the cooling rack. "I've gotta ice some Devil's food cupcakes with the rest of the cream-cheese icing. Wanna give it a shot?"

∼

TWENTY MINUTES LATER, Violet had hand-iced sixty Devil's food cupcakes, each with a Wynne's signature swirl of cream cheese icing. Ben had destroyed a total of six cupcakes attempting to create a swirl similar to Violet's work and still hadn't managed to ice one. He did, however, manage to get tiny globs of icing all over his hands and wrists. With every cupcake he wasted, Violet's tolerance for his clumsiness wore thin; letting out a small grunt under her breath, she looked away as she boxed her finished cupcakes, telling herself that the swirl wasn't easy for everybody. So what if it had only taken her three days to perfect? *Patience, girl, patience.*

When she finally looked up, she noticed he'd gotten a glob of icing on his cheek. "Oh God, Ben—how?"

With a perplexed expression, he asked, "What?"

"You have icing on your face."

Ben grinned shamefacedly, putting down the icing wand and a maimed cupcake.

"Whoops. That's not cute, is it?"

"Not after your first birthday," Violet answered. "You know, you're pretty bad at this, Ben."

He chuckled. "Yeah, this is going to take a while. What's the point of this, anyway? I'm the general manager; why do I need to know how to ice?"

"The more available hands we have to ice, the better.

That way, if there's a cupcake emergency, we'll be able to—"

"*A cupcake emergency?* You can't be serious."

Violet frowned, taking offense at Ben's lighthearted laugh. She didn't enjoy feeling like her passion was being mocked. "I realize it sounds funny, but it's a legit issue. I mean, what happens if one of your white-linen paradises runs out of an item?"

Ben continued wiping icing off his hands and wrists. "We eighty-six the item, period."

"We see more people at this bakery in a day than any of your fine dining establishments see in a week. Eighty-sixing an item isn't an option here. We're ready for anything."

Violet stared at him pointedly, trying to convey the irritation that consumed her. Their eyes finally met, and a strained moment of silence extended between them. All around them customers and counter staff buzzed with life; to Violet, it felt like a tension-filled bubble had just expanded around them and cut them off from the rest of the bakery. She thought it might go on forever, but Ben stepped back.

"You know what, there's a couple of things I have to take care of downstairs. I'll come back up in a little bit."

Violet nodded wordlessly and watched as he made his way past the beverage counter, then the cupcake counter, finally disappearing down the small hallway that led to the steps into the basement. She turned back to the counter with a groan—that didn't go well. She grabbed a trio of chocolate cake layers and vanilla buttercream to ice her next order.

Once she'd completed the orders on her list and it was time to set up the production schedules for the night and overnight bakers and icers, she was completely aware that

Ben hadn't returned. In her mind, he must have planned it that way—the situation got intense and he took off instead of dealing with it. She knew it was because she'd made sure he knew she was offended, and she wouldn't apologize for that. *Well, Ben ol' boy, now you have no choice but to face me.*

She quickly straightened up her station and headed downstairs to the office. Ben was at his seat, facing the door. The receiver of his desk phone was pressed to his ear, and he looked one part mortified, two parts furious. The mix of intense emotion stopped Violet in her tracks. The door shut behind her with a click, and he finally noticed her presence.

Violet caught the brunt of his infuriated gaze and, for one moment, she had no idea whether or not it was meant for her.

"I'm gonna have to call you back." His voice was dark, oddly matching his eyes as they had gone from clear blue to almost stormy.

Ben blindly placed the receiver back onto its cradle while he continued to watch her, waiting for a reaction.

"Is everything all right?" Violet's brow furrowed in concern.

His tense, rigid frame softened slightly. But the emotional wall he was holding up remained. He steadied himself as he prepared to answer, broadening his shoulders in a transparent attempt to get it together. The effect bordered on frightening; Violet's lips parted as her breath silently hitched. Should she walk away?

"I'm fine." His voice remained dark as he turned toward his desk to reach for the apron beside his keyboard.

Violet thought better of pushing the issue, opting simply to say, "Um, okay. I just came down to check in with you. I was hoping to be able to do production and—"

"Okay, look," he said. "It's my second day, and I've got

a lot to learn in terms of administration and operations alone. Do you think you could just handle production and let me do my job before throwing the entire store at me?"

Violet blinked, stunned at the tone he'd taken. "I ... I can, but production is just as important as the—"

"It's dessert, Violet. When all is said and done, it's just cake. I'm sure the world won't end if you press on without me."

She stared at him for a long moment while he very disrespectfully turned his back and threw the apron back on his desk. Dumbfounded, she swallowed a large lump of pride that had begun to swell in her throat. If she disliked anything, it was being spoken down to. But her job was worth much more than the satisfaction of hurling the insults currently threatening to escape her mouth, and she knew it.

"Right." Her face was stony. "Some other time. I'll just go do this upstairs."

"Violet, wait ... "

But she didn't stick around to hear what he had to say. She let the door slam behind her; if it took her an extra hour to do production on the floor, so be it. Violet refused to spend another second of her shift around Ben Preston.

∽

I. AM. Such a jerk.

The words swam in Ben's mind as he crossed West End Avenue and began the walk toward his condo at 160 Riverside Boulevard. He had been impressed with Violet's skills from day one, despite the fact that her knowledge of the bakery made him feel oddly inadequate and unnecessary. By the end of his first day, he wondered why they'd hired him at all, and he mentioned as much to Wynne.

Company Ink

"I'm molding Violet," Wynne had explained. "There's something special in her that could be destroyed if I throw her headfirst into management. She shows a passion for baking that none of my team ever has. I've got a management spot for her in mind, and it's hers when she's ready and I'm ready for her."

"Does she know that?" he asked.

Wynne didn't exactly answer. "She knows how much I value her."

Before Wynne could elaborate, however, she was pulled away to assist with an overcrowded store and a line that wasn't moving. Ben had followed her as she dashed up the stairs from the office and was shocked to find the customer area packed so heavily that members of staff had closed the doors and started a line outside. Jessica, the floor supervisor, was now directing customers out of the side door as they finished paying for their purchases. Violet was helping out at the icing station, cranking out trays of cupcakes faster than anything Ben had ever seen. There were two people stationed at the cupcake counter, and one of them was stuck filling a large order that was rapidly depleting their classic cupcake stores. Ben could only watch from the sidelines as Wynne stepped in and began filling orders at the cupcake counter. He'd never seen this kind of bedlam before.

With the addition of Wynne to the ranks, the situation had resolved itself more quickly than Ben could have imagined, and soon the doors were open again with tourists pouring in for a taste of New York City's most famous desserts. And when it was all over, Wynne calmly led Ben back toward the basement, explaining that these were the kind of fires he'd be putting out from time to time. The thought of what he'd seen happening again brought him right back to feeling inadequate; he could handle a small crowd of people waiting thirty minutes for a table. But hundreds of customers starving for a dozen cupcakes, he wasn't so sure about.

Once again, he was burdened with the reminder that his years of fine dining and his stellar reputation for keeping his bottom line heads and shoulders above the rest didn't seem like enough to make it in Wynne's Kitchen. And the fact that Violet had schooled him earlier in the day did nothing but exacerbate the feeling that he was completely incompetent. He'd already heard about her inexperience; for being there such a short time, Violet was obviously a superstar on a level that he knew he wouldn't be, at least not any time soon. It was that stabbing reality along with bad news from his lawyer in regards to his pending divorce that had made him snap.

He'd regretted being short with Violet the moment he opened his mouth. She was clearly a woman to have on his side. And as he entered his building, he groaned when he thought of how he'd treated her. If he wasn't careful, he'd end up alienating the only other person in the store whose favor actually mattered.

Chapter Three

Ben took long strides into the Pig 'N' Whistle, a long-standing Irish pub on the Upper East Side. It was five o'clock, so the place wasn't yet crowded; he was exhausted from another day at the bakery, but this visit was more business than pleasure. Then again, his brain couldn't have been more filled with nonsense, so he figured a beer would do him good anyway. It only took a cursory glance to spot Tommy, a longtime friend who happened to be doubling as Ben's newly appointed divorce lawyer tonight. He took a seat at the booth, noticing the large manila envelope immediately. He gave Tommy's fist a pound, not taking his eyes off of the envelope.

"So she had the process server bring the papers to you?"

Tommy nodded, pushing a double shot of Johnnie Walker at Ben. "I took a look at the papers. She's coming at you hard, bro."

Ben sipped, welcoming the whiskey's burn as it numbed his throat. "I can imagine. What'd she cite, irreconcilable differences?"

"Actually, she filed for a fault divorce," Tommy answered. "It's the complete opposite of filing based on irreconcilable differences, which most cases are handled under, even the most difficult ones. She's filing on grounds of cruelty and adultery."

Ben responded by tossing back the rest of his drink, closing his eyes as his head swam. "She's trying to ruin me."

"It certainly seems that way," Tommy replied empathetically. "And let me tell you, she doesn't have a single shred of proof unless she knows people willing to lie in court. Either way, it looks like she's going for the jugular."

"Great." Ben sighed. "What's next?"

"Simple. We'll contest her petition and file a countersuit. I can probably even get you out of paying alimony if you can prove somehow that she cheated on you based on that prenup you sent me."

Ben shook his head. "I don't have time for this nonsense, Tommy. I also don't want to spend the next year fighting a battle when all I want to do is get on with my life. I spent seven years funding her entire life, damn it. I'm done."

"I get it. You're pissed off, you're hurting—"

"Of course I am," Ben interrupted with a frown. "But what am I supposed to do? She left me for my best friend and took everything out of the apartment. Then I found out the guy who'd been my lawyer since before I met Elena had been passing information to her the entire time."

"I was wondering why you finally took me up on my offer."

"Well, now you know. My sister's boyfriend, Nate, works at the same firm. He caught Elena having a private meeting with my lawyer. Nate told Lisa, Lisa told me—I called you right after I fired the guy. And here we are."

Company Ink

"Jesus, that's dramatic." Tommy motioned for the waitress. "How are you holding up at the new job?"

Ben shrugged. "Could be better. I was such a jerk to the production supervisor yesterday. She walked in while you and I were on the phone. I couldn't check my attitude, and she caught some of it."

"Easy, bud. You don't wanna end up isolating yourself. Wynne's seems like a real good opportunity for a fresh start."

"Yeah, you're right. I feel horrible, actually. She didn't say a word to me today." "Who?"

"Violet—the production supervisor."

A small smile appeared on Tommy's face. "What's that? Right there, what's that?"

Ben looked perplexed as the waitress swept in and placed two fresh whiskeys in front of them. "What's what?"

"That look in your eye."

Bringing the glass to his lips, Ben said, "I don't know what you're talking about."

Tommy nearly burst into laughter. "Shit, are you into her?"

Ben took a sip and placed his glass on the table. He pursed his lips and remained quiet as he considered whether or not to say anything. Realizing the long moment of silence had already incriminated him, he sighed.

"All right, fine. I might like the girl's work ethic."

"Easy bro," Tommy warned. "Getting involved with a co-worker is a bad idea in the first place, and you're adding divorce to the equation."

"Relax, we're not involved. In fact, I'm pretty sure she hates me. She's this driven, determined thing, and she's full of piss and vinegar."

"As in, she's not falling for your charming restaurant-manager gimmick," Tommy interpreted with a satisfied nod. "What does she look like?"

"Gorgeous, of course," Ben answered wistfully. "Tall, curvaceous, and she's got this wild, black hair. Everything about her screams strong and sexy—she's like a warrior princess with an apron. And can I admit something without you busting my balls?"

"I really can't promise anything."

"She knows how amazing she is," he replied with amusement. "It's not arrogance, though —just confidence. And it scares the hell out of me. She's got a strong personality, and I'm not really sure how to handle it. She's hot, talented, smart—she could have me on the ropes quickly if I'm not careful."

"I can't even rip into you, dude. A woman with a presence like that is kind of scary. I know Elena wasn't like that."

Ben shook his head. "She wasn't. Oh, she talked the talk. But when it came right down to it, she was a bundle of insecurity. Most of the girls I dated were like that anyway."

"And this girl?"

"Violet couldn't care less. And if I said something she doesn't agree with, I'm pretty sure she'd let me have it."

Tommy took a deep swig of his whiskey. "It's just as well. You've got a pretty hard fight ahead of you if we don't come up with a decent strategy."

Ben folded his arms over his chest. "Well then, let's figure this out. Get Elena out of my life."

∽

VIOLET TOOK hesitant steps toward The Rock, not entirely sure she was ready to begin another day. Today would mark Ben's tenth day with the company, and he'd certainly been a challenge. He'd spent about half of his time around her with an attitude the size of Everest. And he'd split the other half between being completely aloof and, on the opposite end of the scale, charming enough to have every single girl in the bakery giggling like idiots. But Violet was exhausted with his back and forth, and she wasn't buying any of it.

He'd walk through the bakery, praising all of the counter staff and eliciting smiles from everyone in the store. In fact, Ben was on his way to being beloved among her co- workers. He'd stop at her station with a smile and ask how her day was going. The first few times she'd engaged happily, discussing the bakery and odd things like breakfast and favorite coffees while he watched her ice special orders. But icing practice with Ben was going as well as if Violet had handed a bucket of buttercream to a two-year-old. Not only was he getting more on his clothes than on the actual cupcake, but the harder she pushed, the sooner he lost interest. He would then disappear into the office and, by the time she got down there to continue his training, he was often tense and irritated.

She'd spent days fighting off the urge to give him as much attitude as he'd given her. She'd also spent days telling herself that she didn't have to go to Wynne—yet. And today, Violet was at the end of her rope. If he didn't at least get his act together where the production schedule was concerned, Violet would pay Wynne a visit at the corporate office. Not one to kick up drama, she strongly hoped she wouldn't have to. But she didn't know what kind of face Ben would be presenting and was beginning to develop the opinion that he was either a phony or a complete lunatic. Whatever the reason for his behavior, she had no time in her life for either. And the last thing she wanted was to be seen as a person who couldn't effectively train someone.

Resigned to a nose-to-the-grindstone mentality for the day, she didn't look up when he walked through the door, and she barely made a sound when he greeted her. Her interaction with Ben throughout the day consisted of no more than a few words, depending on what the situation called for. To her delight, she found the day going by quickly. This would be the best way to deal with Ben's bipolar behavior going forward. And by the time Wynne arrived at two o'clock, Violet was in a much happier mood.

Wynne stepped into the manager's office where Violet was sitting at her desk, surrounded by paperwork with a fresh, hot caramel latte in her hand, her strong, lengthy gams folded beneath her, and her signature wild raven curls sticking out at all angles from the bun at the top of her head. For the first time since Ben started, she was thoroughly at ease. Sensing her mentor's presence, Violet looked up. A wide, happy smile stretched across her face.

"Hi, Wynne!"

Wynne beamed. "Well, hi to you, too! Someone's in a good mood."

"I'm feeling great. How are you?"

"Better now, I think," Wynne replied. "I'll be honest with you. I came down here because Jay was a little worried about a change in your attitude."

Violet could've been knocked over by a feather. "A change in my attitude?"

Wynne took a seat next to her, watching her with a maternal concern. "Jay tells me you've been less exuberant and more introverted. He also tells me that Ben doesn't seem even close to confident with production and … I was just wondering if maybe I'd put a little too much pressure on you."

Company Ink

The tone of Wynne's voice told Violet she was by no means in trouble, but that didn't stop her blood from boiling at Wynne's and Jay's assumption that she was giving less than her all. It was exactly what she'd been concerned about—that Ben wouldn't pick up on the job as fast as Wynne wanted, and it would somehow be Violet's fault.

"He said that, did he?" Stay calm.

Wynne placed a hand on Violet's forearm. "If giving you the task of helping train Ben is too much, it's okay. You've been nothing but a rock star—sometimes it's easy for me to forget that you've only been here a few weeks."

Violet put her pen down, shaking her head gently. "Wynne, I'm not having any problems with my workload. And I would gladly help train Ben if I thought he were at all interested in learning from me."

The words left her mouth before she could stop them; she regretted them less than a second later. She wasn't the type to throw anyone under the bus, but Violet realized quickly that her slightly snarky comment did exactly that. Her eyes closed involuntarily, and she took a deep breath.

"I'm sorry, I didn't mean to say that. I'm sure he's swamped with things that don't involve having a hand in what I do. I know I could definitely teach him more if he'd hang around while I was doing production, but he's being pulled in a lot of different directions."

Wynne smiled. "Don't worry, he's not in any trouble. And don't think for a second that I believe you're giving me anything less than your usual best. That said, a person's first reaction, however blunt and unexpected, is usually the most honest one."

"Wynne, please don't think that I—"

"Vi, relax. These are things I need to know, so I can make sure he gets the training he needs. He's got all of this amazing management experience, so it's important that we all band together to get him to translate his fine dining skills into the bakery. And I don't want revolving-door management. I want someone who will stay with us while we grow. The only way I can control that is to make sure my team is well-trained and happy from top to bottom."

Wynne patted Violet's shoulder affectionately before walking to the office door. Violet watched her uneasily, her forehead pressed against the heel of her hand.

"Trust me, please. I know what I'm doing."

Violet dropped her head into her hands as the office door closed with an ominous thud. She knew all about Wynne's reputation for succinctness as much as anyone in the store did. Ben, however, having spent only a couple of days around the boss, could end up misconstruing her brevity as a reprimand if she happened to mention their conversation. And there was no doubt in Violet's mind that Wynne would mention their conversation. Violet pinched the bridge of her nose with her thumb and forefinger for a moment, letting the tiny pangs of nervousness subside before continuing to look through the online orders to see what she could feasibly add to her own morning schedule before adjusting the evening and overnight lists.

She was just finishing up the production lists for the overnight bakers ten minutes later when Ben stormed into the office. The noisy burst of energy that injected itself into the room made Violet start. She spun around, jolted into a standing position, and was met with Ben's angry, yet somehow devastatingly handsome, glower.

"Are you trying to get me fired?"

Violet's eyes widened in response. "Of course not!"

He certainly looked fit to burst. "What the hell did you say to Wynne?"

"It doesn't matter what I said to Wynne! You're not in trouble, are you?"

"No," he replied, still speaking loudly. "But she questioned my commitment to the company. Is this about production? Are you sabotaging me because I won't spend an afternoon talking cupcakes with you?"

His last few words were dripping with disdain and, frankly, it pissed her off. She placed her hands on her hips and nearly stood on her tiptoes in an effort to be as dominating as he.

"Sabotage? Let me tell you something, homeboy. I don't need to sabotage anybody—I'm one of the most valuable players in the entire company. For that matter, I don't need you to spend the afternoon talking cupcakes, as you so eloquently put it. Wynne thought it would be good for you to be exposed to someone with my pastry background since the bulk of your experience is in upscale restaurants. If you want to figure things out on your own, be my guest!"

"Yes, Violet," he said sardonically. "I want to figure things out on my own!"

"Fine," she replied, the volume of her voice jumping a notch. "Then do that! And while you're at it, you can figure out how to stop being an absolute jerk to me. We're supposed to be on the same team, and you've been nothing but bipolar."

Ben opened his mouth to speak, but ended up closing it. His face contorted from angry to apologetic, and he heaved a heavy sigh. "Okay. You're right. I've been a dick."

Violet stepped back and got a good look at him. She wasn't used to a guy submitting so easily, if you could call ten days of tension easy. "Um, yeah, you have."

He gave her a small, humble smile. His brow furrowed as he dropped his head. "The truth is, I'm going through

... something. I'll admit you might have been catching a little of my anger toward the situation. It was totally misplaced, and I apologize."

Violet could certainly appreciate the added stress that could come with "going through something." But that didn't mean she was on board with his manic behavior, and she wasn't about to allow him to walk all over her, either. Her voice remained firm, even as she felt her angered features soften.

"Can you make this your last apology, please? I'm not working here to be your emotional punching bag and, misplaced or not, your attitude is completely inappropriate."

Ben nodded. "You're right."

"I don't know what you're going through, and I honestly don't care," she continued. "So whatever it is, leave me out of it, okay?"

He took a step closer, closing the gap between them. The chemistry between them ignited effortlessly. Ben was too close for comfort at this point, as he watched her with his head bent. Her breath caught in her throat as she backed up, her butt hitting the edge of the desk. She looked into his face—that gorgeous face—with an air of vague astonishment.

"Friends?" he asked.

She put her hands behind her, gripping the desk for support as the smell of his cologne wafted into her face and nearly sent her cross-eyed. "I don't know. I don't think I can trust you just yet."

Ben smiled. "I promise I'm not a jerk."

"You sure could've fooled me. How about we just take it one day at a time?"

She took a large step to the side, deftly pushing her

Company Ink

chair out of the way with one foot as she created some distance between them.

Ben nodded. "Sounds okay to me. I'll see you tomorrow?"

"Looks like it."

Had something changed between them? Violet couldn't tell. All she knew was that time would tell if he was being honest. She loved working at The Rock, and the last thing she wanted was to be pushed from the store she adored because of her unstable relationship with Ben.

∽

AFTER VIOLET HEADED UPSTAIRS, Ben began to set everything up for the night manager coming in. It had been a long day, one that had left him with a lot to think about. He couldn't shake the guilty feeling that kept washing over him every time he thought of Violet. She didn't deserve to have to deal with the remnants of anger that he'd never be able to aim at Elena. And, until Violet had called him on it, it truly hadn't been something he'd been able to control. He thought that he'd been keeping his head down and his nose clean, but the reality was he'd been going crazy and taking the poor girl with him. Heaving a deep sigh, he decided right there that he'd give Violet a break from here on in.

Regardless of the fact that he'd been dangerously attracted to Violet from the moment he laid eyes on her, the truth was Ben was wary of her, too. She was more than just a pretty face—she was intelligent, strong, and highly ambitious. And the restaurant business, he'd learned over the last ten years, was cutthroat. Experience had also shown him that women in the management track of the industry, having more to prove existing in a male-dominated trade, were shrewd and quite often not to be trusted.

So when Wynne approached him and passively mentioned that he should consider seeing what Violet had to offer in the way of training, he saw red. He was certain she was trying to step on him to get to her rightful place in the bakery. And until he had a second to absorb the genuinely startled look on her face, no one could have told him differently. However, her insistence that she meant no harm triggered something in him. A voice in the back of his head began to tell him that he could trust Violet Young —and it threw him for a loop.

Violet's ability to walk away from him after their brief argument further confused him. Elena seemed to take pleasure in pushing buttons to make sure every disagreement of theirs left them both emotionally exhausted. He was reminded of all the times that he, determined not to argue, would try to walk away from her when she was being particularly dramatic; his refusal to be baited always led to her screaming at him.

"You don't give a shit about me or this marriage!"

"You're such a jerk, Ben!"

"Damn it, Ben! How can you be so *heartless*?"

With a mirthless chuckle, Ben dropped his head in his hands. How hadn't he seen the end of his marriage coming? To this day, he couldn't quite figure out Elena, let alone any woman. But five minutes worth of confrontation with Violet reminded him that all women were not like his soon-to-be ex-wife. Five minutes of conflict was all it took for Ben to see that there was no reason to be upset—this divorce was, literally, the best thing to ever happen to him.

~

Company Ink

VIOLET HAD JUST FINISHED CLEANING up her station. Still in her hairnet and apron, she was leaning forward on the counter as she engaged in conversation about desserts with a friendly and funny mother of two from Minnesota.

"I don't know how you do it," Mrs. Minnesota said with a delighted expression as she looked around at the shelves lined with large, scrumptious-looking cakes. "I've been in line for ten minutes, and it just seems to get crazier!"

"You get used to it," Violet practically shouted over the din, grinning. "And I promise the counter staff is going as fast as they can—I'm so sorry for the wait!"

"Oh please, it's all part of the experience, isn't it? Are you the manager?"

"I'm the production supervisor," Violet replied. "I'm responsible for making sure you guys have plenty of sweets to choose from. Oh, and I ice a few cakes, too."

She loved to throw the icing in as an aside, but the truth was she knew what everyclient's reaction would be when she mentioned that most of the cakes available by 2:00 p.m. were of her own design.

"Did you decorate that lovely carrot cake in the display case?"

"I did, ma'am."

"Well then, that's what we're buying and taking back to the hotel," the customer said matter-of-factly. "I can only hope the good Lord will forgive me for my gluttony this weekend!"

"I'm sure there's some sort of allowance when you're on vacation."

The line finally moved, and Mrs. Minnesota took enough of a leap that Violet had to wave her goodbyes. That last conversation would definitely get her through the rush hour commute with a smile on her face. As Violet put away the last of her tools on a shelf below the countertop, a voice called out to her.

"Excuse me, miss? How much is that Devil's food cake on the top shelf?"

The voice was familiar enough to stop her in her tracks. She turned slowly in the direction of the inquiry. Her eyes caught sight of a familiar face, and she nearly hit the floor. Her hands gripped the counter so tightly that her knuckles went white.

"Steve?"

~

HE LOOKED THE SAME. She was actually sort of pissed that he hadn't grown a hump or become ridden with boils. You know, some sort of physical reminder that he'd been absolutely cruel to her when all was said and done. But there were those eyes like pools of honey and the smile that could charm the pants off a mother superior. Violet stared straight ahead, sitting rigidly straight on the marble fountain across the street from Wynne's. She kept her hands linked tightly in her lap. As long as she didn't look at or touch him, she was fairly certain she could keep herself from falling apart.

Steve leaned forward, forearms on his knees. "You look amazing, Vi."

She kept an eye on the bakery, using it as a source of strength. "It's Violet. And thanks."

Steve smiled at her and scooted closer. "Violet? You always loved it when I called you Vi."

"Well that was before you spent nearly half my inheritance and tried to convince me that I would be lost without you."

She was surprised at how aggressive she'd just sounded.

She may have learned to be stronger as a result of Steve breaking her heart, but she'd never had a chance to actually practice said strength. And she certainly never expected to be able to practice it on him! She'd come much too far from being a heartbroken teenager to let him intimidate her now, so she held on to that fortitude as she met his gaze. He looked … apologetic?

"Okay, I deserved that," he said, flashing a small smile as he tilted his head downward. "And I'm kind of glad you said it. It adds a little to my purpose for being here."

"What purpose is that?"

Steve took a deep breath, releasing a very careful sigh. "I came here to apologize. I was a young, stupid jerk."

"You were sort of a sociopath, actually."

He looked at her with an expression she couldn't quite figure out. Was he remorseful? A nervous feeling set in the pit of her stomach.

"Look, Steve. I don't know what you're actually up here for, but all of this? It just isn't a good idea."

She stood and began to walk away. He was behind her immediately, placing a hand on the small of her back and using the leverage to whip himself in front of her. Now in his arms, she was suddenly visited by the urge to push him into the fountain. He definitely seemed more at ease in their current position than she felt.

"What are you … ?"

Face to face and far too close for comfort, Steve smiled at her. "You still smell like cake."

"Considering I just came out of a bakery, I can't really be impressed at your observation."

He chuckled. "I've missed you."

"I can't say the same."

"Are you trying to push me away?" he asked, a note of teasing in his voice.

"Yes," she replied quickly. "Are you surprised?"

Steve tilted his head and gave her a cheeky grin. "Of course not. But that's only because you've got this image in your head of who I used to be."

"What are you saying? That you've changed?"

"I have," he said, biting his lower lip and meeting her eyes with his own. "Will you meet me for dinner on Friday?"

Violet squirmed out of his grasp. "No, Steve. I don't think that's a—"

"Please, Vi," he begged, grabbing her hands. "I just want to explain myself. I owe you that much, don't you think?"

She sighed. "I just don't think we need to have dinner to bury any hatchets."

"Look, we can catch up, I can officially apologize and then ... who knows?" He reached out to gently twirl one of her curls in his fingers.

She stepped back. "Steve, please—"

"Here," he interrupted again, reaching into his pocket, "take my card. Think about it and call me."

She watched him uneasily as he placed the card in her hand with an overconfident smile. "I'm in town until Saturday. I was hoping to have a chance to try and make up some of what I did to you. Give me a call before Friday afternoon, okay?"

"Um, okay."

He leaned in to kiss her on the cheek, and the familiar scent of sandalwood filled her nostrils. Butterflies erupted in her tummy, and she wasn't sure whether or not it was a good thing. She muttered her goodbyes, and he was gone before she could process what happened. Dinner with Steve. The answer was no—wasn't it? What she did know was that his reappearance couldn't be a good thing.

Chapter Four

*B*en stood by the front door of the condo as men dressed in coveralls with the Jennifer Convertibles logo on their breast pockets carried in a complete living room set, piece by piece. The sight of his living room finally taking shape made him heave a sigh of relief; it had been far too long since he'd felt normal.

"Mr. Preston?" The older of the three delivery guys setting up the living room gave Ben a cautious look. "We're bringing the entertainment unit up now along with the dinette set for the kitchen, and that'll be it. Are you sure you don't want us to hang the frames?"

"No, it's fine. I need something to do later on tonight. Can I get you guys a couple of bottles of water for the road?"

"That'd be great, thanks. We'll be right back up."

"Sure thing. Just leave the door open." Ben headed back to the kitchen.

The management company that owned the building had put in brand new, state-of-the- art appliances and cognac-colored maple cabinets when they first moved in. He and Elena had added a dinette set that had perfectly matched the cabinets. Ben loved having breakfast at that dinette; serving up something delicious to go with their morning coffee had been his favorite morning ritual. The kitchen used to look lived in. Now, with Elena having emptied it of its character, the kitchen masqueraded as a brand new room. A slight pang hit him in the gut, and he couldn't decide if it was because of Elena or the dinette.

Just as he grabbed a few bottles of water, he heard the faint sound of footsteps in the living room. Thinking it was awfully soon to be returning with an entertainment unit, a table, and four chairs, he stepped carefully toward the front of the condo. He turned into the living room's entrance and paused, his stomach sinking. There stood Elena, her chestnut hair swept into a stylish twist, and wearing business attire that almost made him miss the curves of her body. Elena's eyes met his for the first time since she left the condo—and boy, if looks could kill …

After a long moment of tense silence, Elena was the first to speak. "I'm surprised to see you here."

"I live here."

Elena gave him a smug smile. "Really? When you should be saving your money for alimony?"

Ben pursed his lips, fighting back the stream of curses. "That's awfully presumptuous."

"Is it? The way I see it, I've got a lot coming to me."

"No arguments there. But assuming you'll see a penny in alimony is just … ballsy."

She folded her arms. "After all you put me through? Alimony's a small price, Ben."

"Okay, here's where I'm confused. You spent God knows how many years sleeping with Ethan behind my back, yet you're telling everyone with ears that I put you through hell. What did I actually do to you?"

Elena ignored his question as she turned on her heel to look around the living room. "This furniture is hideous."

"You never liked anything I picked out," Ben retorted, watching her as she approached the infamous lampshade as it lay defenseless on his brand new plush, chocolate-colored sofa. "Is that part of what I did wrong?"

She picked up the lampshade before slowly facing him again. "You'll never understand. But I promise you, I will make you as miserable as you made me. And everyone's going to know what you did."

Ben couldn't help but chuckle. "Well, then hopefully they'll clue me in. Because I still have no idea what I could have possibly done that would have compelled you to spread your legs for a guy like Ethan."

Elena glared as if she were willing lasers to shoot from her eyes. "I hate you, Ben Preston."

Ben raised an eyebrow. "Obviously. I'll see you in court."

∽

VIOLET HAD SPENT NEARLY two days wondering what could have possessed Steve to come all the way up to New York City to track her down. Was his appearance really as simple as an apology, or did he have an ulterior motive? For hours on end, she went over the last moments of their relationship, telling herself that he didn't actually deserve an opportunity to apologize, whether he was being sincere or not. As a result, she didn't bother to give him an answer.

But Steve, apparently, was determined to charm her into dinner. He'd sent her multiple text messages since popping back into her life on Wednesday and remained steadfast through Thursday morning, despite the fact that she hadn't once answered him. Now, on Thursday afternoon, Violet was spending as much of the last half of her shift in the office at Wynne's Kitchen as she could, simply because there was no cell phone signal in the basement. Barely able to focus, she sat in the office by herself tapping out a rhythmless beat with her pen on the desk. She had finished production and made the lists for the overnight shift and the following day.

Violet knew she was stalling and had quickly run out of reasons to remain downstairs. She couldn't even use Ben as an excuse anymore; since their confrontation, he'd actually been pretty pleasant to her. She probably wasn't a pleasure to be around at this point, but she was doing her best to conceal her anxiety. The truth was, she didn't want to deal with any of this head-on again. She'd walked away from Steve when it counted, hadn't she? Why should she have to face him twice? What the hell did he want now?

Behind her, the door opened. Violet was a little disgusted that, somehow, her ears readily recognized the way Ben's feet hit the floor as he entered the office. She picked her head up quickly and stared at her computer screen, doing her best to feign interest in a handful of Seamless orders that she'd already added to the production schedule.

"Everything okay down here?" he asked.

"Just fine, Ben," she answered quickly, her voice barely louder than a whisper.

She could hear him shift his stance so that he was facing her. "Are you sure? I haven't seen you on the floor in about an hour."

"I finished my list. I took a few special orders, and then

Company Ink

I came down here to take care of the baker's schedules," she replied through clenched teeth. "Is something wrong upstairs?"

"Not at all. But I did see you with your head in your hands, so I figured you might have been a little stressed. Did I say or do something to offend you?"

She sighed, feeling her patience being tested in a big way. "No, Ben. Believe it or not, you're not my only source of stress and anxiety."

Ben chuckled in response. "Ah, so you *aren't* always a sweetheart—I was beginning to worry you were too perfect to actually be human."

"Well, you already brought it out in me once before, so why would you be surprised now?"

"You know, Violet, I've really been trying with you these last couple of days. It's pretty hypocritical of you to ride my ass for projecting onto you when it seems like all you've done since we last talked is project on me."

His words stung. And of course, she lashed out. "What can I say? My attitude reflects the store's leadership ... *sir*."

"Really, Vi? You're telling me *this* is you?"

She spun around in her seat, jerking herself into a standing position. "It's Violet, and don't think I don't feel you hovering over me like you're trying to prove yourself as my lord and master. I don't care how big you are—I'm not afraid of you, okay?"

"Um, okay."

"You seem to think that because you're twelve feet tall, I'm supposed to be concerned about what you think of me. I may not be able to look you in the face, but I ... you know what?"

In a move that even she wouldn't be able to explain later, she grabbed a nearby folding chair and opened it.

She then slid it in front of Ben so that it nearly hit his shins and, without a single rational thought, stood on it so that she could stare him in the face.

Ben's shoulders rose in a silent chuckle as he avoided her gaze. "Well, now I know that you're *not* all right. Do you realize what you're doing right now?"

Violet's brow furrowed, and she looked down, catching on to the magnitude of her foolish display. Her cheeks burned. "Um, maybe I didn't think this through."

Ben smiled widely at her. "I appreciate your fiery display here, but you're forgetting that I am taller than you and … " Without warning, he leaned forward slightly and threw her over his shoulder.

Violet let out a quick, sharp scream; she grabbed on to his shoulders with a grunt and tried to straighten herself, nearly hitting her head on the low ceiling.

"Despite the fact that we're in a place of business, I have no problems reminding you of that."

Her eyes widened as she absorbed the fact that she was unceremoniously hanging from his long, lean body. Although, looking downward, she could see the firm bottom she'd admired when they first met nearly two weeks ago.

Ben chuckled, his laugh deep and playful. "Are you calm enough? Or are you going to punch me in the face if I put you down?"

"Put me down, Ben. *Now.*"

He set her down, and Violet gave him a stern look before reaching back and slapping him across the face. He paused, closing his eyes for a moment as he accepted her reaction. He then nodded.

"Yeah, I deserved that."

Violet folded her arms and spoke calmly. "This is obvi-

Company Ink

ously not working out. I'll ask Wynne for a transfer by the end of the week."

Without another word, she walked past him and threw the office door open. The night manager, Jamie, stood at the threshold, a shocked expression on her face.

"Vi, was that you? I heard a scream."

"I thought I saw a mouse under my desk. But it was just a hat."

Violet made her way through the prep area without waiting for the night manager's reply. Up the stairs to the main floor she headed, past the cupcake counter and onto the sales floor. She was pulling her cell phone out of her pocket as she ignored the floor supervisor calling her name. The phone was to her ear as she pushed past the crowds of tourists, and there was no turning back as she tugged on the front entrance and headed into the open air.

"Hey, it's Vi. Still up for dinner tomorrow?"

～

FRIDAY FLEW by in a haze for Ben. The pace, while he'd managed to keep up without getting overwhelmed, had kept him far too busy to have anything more than a yes/no conversation with Violet. And he knew he owed her more than that. A bridge had burned between them after he'd dominated her the day before, and it hadn't taken more than an hour for him to realize that he messed up and would've given anything to take back what he'd done in the heat of the moment. In fact, he had spent the entire day waiting to hear from Wynne, who would certainly have a problem with her protégé wanting to transfer out of the company's flagship location.

The call from Wynne never came, however. Had Violet changed her mind about leaving? On more than a couple of occasions, he caught himself watching her at the icer's station from the registers, hoping he hadn't destroyed any shot he had of building something good with the bakery by pissing off the one girl he'd been excited about working with from the moment he met her.

His entire commute home to his Upper West Side condo was spent thinking of her, wondering how he could possibly turn things around. Even after showering and heading back out to meet Tommy at Hiro Sushi, he couldn't shake the thought of her upset or his own feelings of guilt that followed.

Ollie's Hiro Sushi was a small, chic but casual Chinese/Japanese restaurant located less than a couple of blocks from Ben's building, tucked away on the corner of Freedom Place and West Sixty-Eighth Street. As he followed the waitress to his table, he couldn't help but acknowledge the irony. He and Elena had spent many nights huddled in a random booth around a bottle of wine, making out between courses like a couple of lovesick teenagers. Now he was here waiting for his attorney to arrive so that he could discuss the details of his divorce, along with a strategy to stop the woman he'd once loved from destroying his life.

He'd already drained one whiskey and had been swirling the second in its glass for what felt like a long time before his phone finally rang.

"Bro, it's Tommy. Where are you?"

"Exactly where I told you I'd be," Ben answered. "At Ollie's, waiting for you."

"Shit. I'm guessing you didn't get my message, then."

Ben fought off the frustrated sigh that threatened to escape. "That'd be a fair assumption."

"I've got a pretty hefty emergency with another client,"

Company Ink

Tommy said. "They pay by the hour and your case is pro bono, so ... "

"I get it. So why are you calling?"

"To check in. And to make sure you're not pissed at me."

"I wasn't when I thought you were coming."

Tommy groaned. "Come on, bro, I'm sorry. I have bills to pay, ya know? I followed up with my contact to make sure I'm not missing anything from Elena's camp, and it's cool. Nothing's changed yet, at least not for the worse."

"Elena's camp," Ben repeated. "What kind of assault is she building, anyway? And who's your contact? Because I don't think I've ever heard you mention their name."

"I can't yet," Tommy replied quickly. "The person I've been chatting with could destroy Elena's case against you, and I'm still in the process of wearing them down. If it got back to her that I was working on someone so close, it'd destroy everything."

"This is all way too Mission Impossible for me. What happened to the days when a guy and girl could just get divorced and call it a day?"

"No one told you to marry a delusional lunatic, pal." Tommy chuckled, his voice hardened and reminiscent of a gangster film. "She's built you up in her mind to be some sort of monster, and she's made the act of divorcing you into some sort of conquest. I've read some of her statements and trust me, bro—you don't want to know."

"But I do! Why haven't I seen these papers yet?"

"Would you trust me, please? I'm handling this ... You don't need any more of the stress."

"Dude, we need to talk about this." Ben ran a hand through his hair in exasperation. "I'm tired of the secrets and the sheltering. I feel like you're pulling me through a minefield with my eyes closed."

"All right, Ben, you win. I'll show you everything," Tommy conceded. "Except my source. I can't risk Elena finding out."

"Fine, that's a deal," Ben agreed. "But I'll tell you what, if you can get me out of this with little to no collateral damage, I'll make it worth your while."

Tommy laughed. "Don't paint yourself into any corners, buddy. But you know I've got your back."

"All right, I've got a Scotch to nurse." Ben sighed. "Maybe I'll drink myself stupid and stumble back to my place. Lord knows I'm close enough to make it."

"Yep, that's healthy. Just be careful, all right? Try to avoid doing anything stupid."

"I make no promises."

As Ben wrapped up the call, he spotted something shiny out of the corner of his eye. The shiny something happened to be a silver bangle, but it was the arm to which it was attached that made his heart skip a beat. *Violet?* He set his phone down without looking, dangerously close to dropping it in his glass. What was Violet doing in his neighborhood? It occurred to him that he had no idea where she lived.

Her eyes darted nervously around the restaurant, and his stomach churned as he dropped his head to avoid being seen. Maybe she's meeting someone, but here? Mercifully, the waitress approached as he struggled to get his thoughts together, batting her eyes and smiling.

"Can I get you another Scotch, sir?"

He twisted in his chair so that the waitress was directly in front of him. "Sure. Why don't you tell me what you recommend?"

Ben hardly heard her launch into details about their top-shelf product. He smiled up at her and nodded, all the while peeking around the waitress to glance at Violet, who

Company Ink

seemed thoroughly engrossed in the menu her server had placed at her table.

"Sir?" *Whoops.* He hadn't heard her stop talking.

"You know what, I think I'll just stick to what I've got here," he replied, feeling guilty. "But thanks."

He eyed Violet from across the restaurant, carefully keeping his head tilted toward his glass. He noticed she was tense and obviously nervous—her hands, knotted together, practically tapped out a rhythm on the table as she sat with her eyes closed and took deep breaths. A small twinge of jealousy that he refused to acknowledge set up a knot in the pit of his stomach. *Hot date, huh?* He tossed back the last sip of his second Scotch just as the waitress served up his third, whisking the other glass away without so much as a word. Violet's server approached her table with a smile but was turned away with a nervous shake of the head as Violet buried her face in her menu.

He had gone through his third drink and was just being brought another when Violet's demeanor finally changed. She repeatedly checked her phone, alternatively staring out the window, fiddling with her silverware, and looking through her menu. Then, with a final check of the phone, her shoulders slumped. Ben grabbed his own and looked at it; an hour had gone by. And he'd been watching her like a stalker for exactly that long. With a frown, he realized that Violet had been stood up. His brow furrowed as he watched sympathetically—she stared hard at the tablecloth in front of her, and Ben could tell that she was willing herself not to cry. And before he could stop himself, he was out of his chair and fast approaching her table.

"Violet?"

She looked up with a startled expression. "Ben? What are you ... ?"

"I live in the neighborhood," he said casually. "Just stopping in for dinner. Do you live around here?"

She took a breath before replying, "No, not at all. I was, um … I am meeting someone."

"Oh." He nodded, feigning ignorance. "I'm guessing they'll be here any minute then?"

"Actually," she sniffed, standing, "I think I've been stood up. So I think I might just…"

He held out a hand to stop her from grabbing her purse. "Wait, would you maybe …? Do you think you might want to have a drink?"

Violet froze, obviously surprised by his abrupt invitation. Ben, frankly, was about as stunned by his offer as she looked. But he couldn't leave her there by herself—the disappointment on her face and the embarrassment in her eyes knocked him for a loop. Compared to the strong cake-queen persona she always had on display for him at work, this current vulnerability took him by surprise, and his heart immediately went out to her. *One drink can't hurt. Maybe I can send her home with a smile.*

"I mean," he continued, "before you go, of course. Come on, I owe you one."

"That's really nice of you, Ben," she answered cautiously. "But I think I'll just …"

Ben stepped around her and pulled her chair out slightly, gesturing toward it. "Come on, just one. At least let me ease my conscience."

Violet heaved a sigh and took the chair he offered, scooting with its movement as he tucked her back into the table.

"What are you drinking?" he asked as he took the seat across from her. She folded her hands in her lap. "The house Merlot."

Company Ink

"That's a heavy red for the summertime," he remarked. "You like big wines, I take it?"

She nodded. "I'm not much of a connoisseur, obviously. But I like my wine to have a punch, I guess. The Chardonnays and the Pinot Grigios just aren't my thing."

Ben smiled. "I can respect that."

He called the waitress over and ordered another Scotch for himself and a glass of Merlot for her. Violet gave him an impressed look, a teasing grin stretching across her face.

"Talk about heavy drinks for the summertime. I'd be sweating like an animal if I had what you're drinking."

Slightly offended, he frowned. Was she putting the walls back up? "I wasn't judging your choice of wine, was I?"

"No, and I wasn't either ... I was just ... I was just saying." Violet dropped her head with a small, embarrassed smile.

"So, Violet"—he was careful to use her full name as she had corrected him so many times before—"do you live anywhere near here?"

She shook her head. "Washington Heights. Well, I'm right at the border. I was just down here meeting someone for dinner."

"Ah, the dummy who stood you up."

She bit her lip nervously and nodded. "Yeah, that guy. It's fine, though. He won't get another shot now."

The hard anger in her voice as she dismissed her potential suitor made Ben cringe a little, and he laughed in spite of himself. "Wow, remind me not to get you angry."

Violet tilted her head to one side, finally looking good-natured. "You already did, remember?"

"You got me there, Violet." Ben slumped in defeat, and she let out a peal of delighted laughter.

"Call me Vi."

Their eyes locked, and a warm stretch of silence extended between them as the server placed their drinks in front of them. Once again, it may as well have been day one. Glad that he hadn't decided to call it an early night, Ben found his appetite—among other things—returning. And, if he were being honest with himself, Violet was certainly a great alternative to an early, whiskey-sodden bedtime.

Chapter Five

Three hours, dinner, and quite a few drinks later, Violet was surprised to have learned as much about him as she had in this short span of time. They'd traded life stories over truly scrumptious dim sum and a shared plate of lo mein. Their check sat unattended on the table between them. She drained her umpteenth glass and licked her lips while she studied him. Her tummy jumped as he watched her quietly.

"Well, forgive me for saying so," she remarked, "but Elena sounds like a nut job."

"As does Steve. I'm sorry you had to go through that."

"So am I." She nodded, waving for the server. "And I'm sorry you had such a cold-hearted witch for a wife. If I had been in her shoes, things would have been a lot different."

Yikes. Maybe that was a little too forward for a girl who'd only been friendly with him for the equivalent of a full day. Too late to hold her tongue now. She looked up at Ben self-consciously; his smile had widened.

"Don't get shy on me now, Vi. This is easily the most open and fun conversation I've had in … years."

She sucked her teeth. "Oh, come on, Ben … years?"

He nodded. "I've got no reason to lie. I've had an absolute blast hanging out with you tonight. And honestly? I don't want it to end."

She sat back in her chair and crossed her arms, grinning boldly. "You mean that, don't you?"

He brought his glass to his lips. "Like I said, I've got no reason to lie."

Ben continued to watch her, his gaze playfully dark as he drained his glass. She hadn't expected her night to turn out like this, but here she was. And where it was headed was obvious, at least in her mind. She bit her lower lip again, butterflies setting up camp in her tummy and sending tiny bolts of lightning through her veins. She took a deep breath and exhaled loudly, amused by just how unready she was for all of this.

"Oh man, I hate to do this," she said, "but I have to go. I just really—I can't."

Ben paused and nodded. "I get it. But can I see you again?"

She stood slowly, and he followed suit. Was he being a gentleman, or was he just too drunk to realize what he was doing? He approached her with a flirtatious smirk, his steps resembling a cowboy's swagger that had the potential to drive her crazy. She ran a hand through her untamed tresses, grabbing a handful as she laughed coyly.

"You mean like at work … boss?"

Ben dropped a rather large bill onto the table with a chuckle, and Violet pretended hard not to notice the tremendous tip he was leaving as he led her away from the table. "Oh, I was hoping that wouldn't come up tonight."

"How could it not come up? You're my manager; I'm your production supervisor."

"We're two people who seem to get along a lot better when we're not at the bakery." Ben placed one hand directly on her back as he reached forward and held the door open for her with one strong, deft arm. "But you're right. It might be a problem—I've never been interested in a co-worker before."

Violet strolled toward the curb, her head swimming from the copious amounts of wine she'd imbibed. A happy giggle escaped her lips, and she nearly clamped her hands over her mouth. "Me neither."

Oh no. A twinge of panic rushed through her as their arms brushed together. Ben was her boss; getting involved with him was a bad idea, period. This should have been an easy decision. Instead, Violet felt like she was being tugged in opposite directions by both arms.

She watched as he took long strides to the curb, his long and graceful body extending outward as he hailed a cab. He was wearing a black v-neck tee shirt and dark blue jeans, and she noticed for the first time that his blond locks were perfectly mussed. Maybe it was the Merlot goggles, but Ben Preston was more gorgeous than she remembered. A cab came screeching to a stop in front of them, and she immediately regretted saying she had to leave. She dropped her head with a sigh and stepped toward the cab, looking up to say goodbye. To her surprise, Ben was closer than ever and still taller by a large amount despite the fact that she was standing on the curb and he was in the street.

"Wow," she breathed. "You're ... really tall."

"Yes, ma'am." Ben sniffed playfully.

And you smell like heaven. But all she could mutter was, "Like, really tall."

"Is that all you have to say?"

Violet could feel her cheeks burning as she watched Ben examine her face carefully. The world around her seemed to fall into a haze; the only things left were his ice-blue eyes, chiseled jaw covered in a half day's growth, and that far too tempting mouth.

Ben reached out, touching her jaw with a gentle, slightly callused fingertip. "Vi?"

"Hmm?"

"The cab is here."

Thoroughly embarrassed, she took a careful step off the curb. "Ben, it's been …"

"It has."

She swallowed a lump in her throat. "Will you …?"

He smiled warmly, curving his finger beneath her chin. "Tomorrow."

Her heart raced and her breath grew short—they may have connected to the point that he was actually reading her mind. *What the hell is going on?* Before she could declare to herself for the second time that night that this wasn't like her, Ben tilted her chin upward. Her lips parted involuntarily and, without another word, his mouth closed over hers. The kiss was gentle, unassuming … *genuine*. It was unlike anything she'd ever experienced, and her entire body was humming by the time he pulled away from her.

Violet closed her eyes, dropping her head with a sigh as her indecisiveness came to a crashing halt. It may have been completely unlike her, but she couldn't shake the feeling that if she didn't speak now, the opportunity may never present itself again.

"Get in the car."

"Excuse me?"

"Just get in the cab," she replied with a nervous smile, "before I change my mind."

Company Ink

He extended his arm toward the open door. "Ladies first."

Every nerve ending in her body was tingling in excitement. The effects of the wine had made her brave beyond belief, but she knew there was no way she'd regret this in the morning. She climbed into the cab and scooted over to the far side.

"Take us to 143rd and Broadway, please. Quickly."

She pressed her back against the car door as Ben reached for her, his eyes filled with mischief. Violet couldn't help but give a nervous chuckle as his mouth claimed hers again. She was beneath him in the back seat of the cab, only partially aware that there was someone else in the car. Ben's hands found their way just under the edge of her shirt; slender fingers danced along the curves of her waist and moved toward the small of her back. She wrapped her arms around his neck and giggled beneath his lips.

He smiled but kept his lips against hers. "Ticklish?"

She sighed as he moved his mouth away to nip at her neck and responded, "Only for the moment."

His breath against her ear ignited a fire in the pit of her tummy. "You smell like cupcakes."

"Do you like it?" she asked, her voice trembling.

"More than I did the first time we met." The tip of his tongue flicked its way across the pulse point behind her ear. "And I liked it then."

For a brief moment she was thankful that she was already lying down, because the sound of his voice made her weak at the knees. Feeling encouraged, she reached up,

running her hand up the back of his head and grabbing a handful of his straight, blond locks, so soft to the touch. She tugged his head. His eyes rolled back, and a moan escaped his lips. She may have liked the giddy schoolgirl feeling she got when he kissed her, but she wasn't one to stay underneath a guy for long.

Ben gave in willingly as she pushed against him and forced herself into a sitting position. His eyes darkened as she straddled him, and his already mischievous grin stretched across his face just a bit more as Violet displayed her more aggressive side. She tugged his head back again and allowed herself a moment to nibble on his neck and collarbone. Her dominance turned him on, judging by his breathlessness and the rapidly growing bulge pressing against her jeans.

Ben gripped her tightly by the hips as the cab picked up speed on the West Side Highway. Violet gasped against his mouth as his hands made their way further up her back, beneath her shirt. A low growl settled in the bottom of his throat as his hands found the clasp of her bra; within seconds, it popped open. She pulled away from him with a startled squeak, her eyes wide as she let out a delighted laugh.

"Somebody's fast," she teased, scooting closer to him in a thinly veiled attempt to rub against his massive erection.

"Well, you did say you were likely to change your mind," he joked, reaching up her shirt sleeves and deftly maneuvering her bra straps down.

She allowed Ben to pull the straps off of her arms, and it only took another moment to pull it out from under her shirt entirely.

"I'll just take this." He stuffed the bra into his pocket, and she threw her head back and laughed. With expert fingers, he tugged the front of her shirt outward and snuck a peek.

"Impressive," he murmured.

"I like 'em."

Ben chuckled again and leaned forward, placing an

affectionate kiss over her heart. Her breath caught in her throat, the out-of-place but terribly sexy gesture taking her by surprise. The car came to a stop and idled in front of her apartment building.

"Thank God," she said breathlessly, opening the car door and stepping out.

Thankful she hadn't tripped over anything climbing off of Ben, she reached into her purse. But he was already on the sidewalk next to her, having handed the cab driver the fare plus a pretty hefty tip. He pulled her close, tilting her chin towards him with a curled index finger. She felt her knees go weak and nearly went down before he hooked her against him by the waist and kissed her. *Oh boy*, she thought nervously as Ben's hand slid up the back of her shirt. *Let the dipping commence.*

~

VIOLET'S APARTMENT door opened abruptly, and they spilled in, attached at the mouth as she struggled with the lock. Her purse hit the floor a few feet away from the door, and she managed to get his belt and top button undone before Ben pulled her shirt over her head. She tugged at his v-neck, and he obliged by quickly taking it off. Violet wasted no time, letting her hands run over his torso as they kissed. She pushed him against the wall with a soft thud and wrapped her arms around his neck. He let out an involuntary groan, and with a small hop she wrapped her legs around his waist. His hands cupped her bottom as he walked through the living room and toward the hallway.

"The first door to the left," she moaned against his mouth.

"Mmm," he responded, opening her door with a gentle kick.

Ben took a knee at the foot of the bed and lowered her, slowly, onto the mattress beneath him. Her fingers were tangled in his hair as they kissed, and he took the time to yank her jeans down, over her hips, and around her knees. Violet made a few jerky moves he couldn't understand, until he realized she was kicking her shoes off. He stood to remove his pants as she lifted her legs high in the air to remove her own.

He marveled at the sight before him. Clad in nothing but a pair of red lacy boy shorts that matched the bra still in the pocket of his discarded jeans, Violet's body was built for trouble. Her wild, raven curls were fanned out on the bed; her slender neck led a perfect path to a small but perfectly shaped bosom that looked as delicious as her well-rounded hips. She carefully ran a hand down her soft, flat tummy, watching him as he watched her. She let her fingertips stop just beneath her panties, waiting for him to urge her on. Ben licked his lips, slowly dropping to his knees between her parted thighs.

"Do you taste as good as you look?" he asked, his voice husky.

"You tell me."

He smirked, letting out a growl as he hovered over her exposed breasts. He placed a soft, teasing kiss at the hollow of her throat, and Violet tilted her head back. The tip of his tongue danced slowly down the center of her chest. He cupped the underside of her left breast while he continued his oral assault on her torso. He settled his pelvis between her legs and pressed his erection against her sex. She pushed her hips upward to meet him, and he wished there were a faster way to get their underwear off. His tongue began its descent toward her most private of areas, forcing a melodic moan from her lips; hands on his shoulders, she gently urged him lower.

"Please, Ben," she sighed.

"Tell me what you want, Vi."

Heavy-lidded, she answered, "Your face, between my legs. Now."

He planted a kiss just below her belly button before murmuring against her skin, "My pleasure."

She quivered as he backed up, pulling her panties down as he went. She bent her knees as she lay and ran trembling hands from her breasts to her lower abdomen. He could tell she was nervous; he wouldn't admit that he was, too, because they had already changed everything. And there would be no regrets tonight. He leaned down and planted a feathery kiss on the backs of her hands as they gripped her sheets. He looked up, noticing that her eyes had closed, a small smile forming on her face as her cheeks turned pink.

"No, Vi," he instructed. "Watch me."

Her eyes opened, and her gazed focused first on his face, then his hands.

"Perfect." He grinned.

~

PRESSING GENTLY on the inside of her knees, Ben spread her legs apart, revealing her sex. He left a trail of nibbling kisses against her inner thigh as he made his way hungrily toward her silken folds. Violet's breath caught in her throat as his mouth hovered briefly over its final destination. And when his mouth finally made contact, her back arched in response. Violet drew in a sharp breath, letting out a desperate moan as he paused to nibble on her inner thighs, his mouth brushing against her sex as he passed from one leg to the other. She grabbed a handful of his hair and lifted her pelvis to his mouth, demanding more.

As Ben's tongue continued to tease her, Violet's hips began to move of their own accord. She silently urged him on, her breathing labored as she swayed against his mouth. She delighted in the sound of his satisfied moan, and her body reacted to the rhythm his tongue had set as it swept against her. The vibration from Ben's chuckle made Violet twitch and throb, her wetness increasing as his tongue probed her skillfully. Violet felt the climax coming, like a freight train picking up speed. Expertly, Ben's tongue and fingers worked their magic; she tried to watch him, to give him what he asked her for. But she had already lost control, wanting nothing more than to fall off the jagged edge to which he had quickly brought her.

Finally, she climaxed—a moan escaped her lips in a crescendo, and she gasped as waves of intense release washed over her again and again. Onward he continued, suckling and nibbling as she contracted and pulsed against his willing mouth. Expecting to come down from the high, her hips twitched away from him. She gasped in surprise as he wrapped his arms around her hips, pinning Violet to the bed and his face to her. Ben continued his delicious assault, invoking delighted sounds from Violet as he expertly took her right back to the edge of release.

"Ben," she moaned, slowing grinding against him.

He had no problems matching her urgency, pinning her down with one arm as he freed his fingers to insert first one, then two, deep in her core.

"Mmm," he moaned as she contracted around his fingers. "So tight."

She panted as his whisper of a remark pushed her over the edge again. Violet whimpered as her vision went blurry and she lost all sense of time, surfing an orgasmic wave

Company Ink

more intense than the first. His mouth left her; Violet sighed, thinking to herself that nothing could feel as amazing as this. That is, until she felt Ben hovering over her; without warning, he entered her—slow, deep, complete. Her back arched, and she gasped.

He filled her over and over, his manhood nestling inside of her. She matched his passionate thrusts, and he grabbed her hands, lacing their fingers together as he buried his face in her neck. She lifted her legs and, to her delight, he went deeper; he moaned her name in exclamation, his head tilting backward as he thrust harder in response. Wanting so much more, she lifted herself against him and maneuvered herself on top of him. Ben was now pinned beneath her, his shoulders pressed into the bed as she gyrated against him. Back and forth she rocked, reveling in the feeling of his thick member inside of her. She felt him throb and pulse against her walls, and she knew he was near his apex. Their rhythm quickened again, and he sat up to grab a hold of her bottom and draw her closer. She wrapped her arms around his neck, using the leverage to widen the movement of her hips. She leaned back slightly as his eyes rolled backward.

"Come for me," she said, her voice demanding as she continued to grind against him.

Her command sent him over the edge, and he thrust deeply, one final time, as his body went rigid. She held on to him with her head pressed against his shoulder, waiting for her heart to stop racing. Ben placed a kiss on her collarbone as he lifted her off of him easily, placing her gently on the bed beside him. He pressed his lips to hers, his kiss lingering, and Violet let out a small giggle.

"A giggle isn't really what a guy wants to hear after what he thought was pretty amazing," he remarked with a smirk.

"No, no," she replied, letting out another giggle as he wrapped his muscular arms around her and pulled her close. "That's not what I ... I mean, it was incredible! But I can't help thinking we've just made matters worse at work."

He nuzzled her neck. "Right. As in, how am I supposed to argue with the hardheaded supervisor when I can't keep my hands off of her?"

"Hardheaded. That's going a little overboard, isn't it?"

Ben's expression was comically bewildered. She tilted her head back and let out a laugh.

"All right, all right! Hardheaded. But you weren't easy to deal with either."

"That's true. But now you know I wasn't being rude on purpose." He patted her behind affectionately. "I was too busy trying to ignore your amazing ass."

She chuckled again. "Well, it isn't Shakespeare, but ... Tomorrow should be interesting."

Chapter Six

Ben left her house about an hour before her alarm went off. They kissed goodbye with a promise to have dinner again on Friday night, and she closed her apartment door behind him with a sigh of relief. The last thing she wanted was to play Who Walks in First?, that awkward game a couple plays when they're co-workers scheduled for the same shift after a night-long secret tryst. *Worse than the walk of shame*, she thought as the picture of Ben taking a cab home wearing clothes that had spent an entire evening on the floor of her bedroom swirled through her mind. Her heart pounded as she padded gingerly toward the bathroom to run the shower.

She knew the last thing she should have ever done was bring Ben home. She had a career to build with Wynne's Kitchen, and fraternizing with management was a definite red-ink mark on her employee record. But she couldn't find an ounce of regret, even as the thought of keeping last night a secret incited intense feelings of guilt.

She let the hot water run over her face. She could still feel the weight of his hands and the feathery touch of his kisses on her skin; her body reacted with wave after delicious wave of longing. Being with Ben felt surprisingly right; Violet had no idea what lay beyond this week for them, but she couldn't wait to find out.

Ben was already in the office when she arrived, and the sales floor was bustling with the sound of the morning counter staff laughing and socializing as they set up towers of muffins and scones, trays of cupcakes, and platters of various cookies and bars for the a.m. rush. Violet went for her usual cup of coffee when Jay, the operations manager who'd been assigned to keep a close eye on Ben's progress, approached her.

"Good morning, doll," he said in a playful tone.

"Hiya, Jay. What's up?"

He smiled, the tip of his tongue touching his upper lip. "What's up? You tell me. You just came in glowing like a UV light."

"I don't know what you're talking about."

"Oh, we're playing that game? Okay, that's cool. But when you're ready to tell me who you rode to work on this morning, I'll be right over by the registers."

Violet dropped her head with a smile as Jay sauntered away. They had hit it off from day one, and she liked the sweet but sarcastic operations manager. But Jay loved to tease people and, if Violet weren't careful, he'd unravel the secret. *No after-work drinks with Jay*, she noted mentally as she headed down to the office to pull online orders that had come in overnight.

Her tummy did backflips in anticipation as she inched closer to the manager's office. Violet urged herself to remain calm, cool, and collected, but how was she supposed to act like nothing happened around a guy who'd just spent hours between her legs the night before? Flashes of Ben lifting her off the bed as he thrust into her deeply

Company Ink

ignited fireworks in her core. Violet held on to the doorknob to the office for a moment, forcing herself to take a deep breath. Surely Ben was on the other side telling himself the same thing. With a flick of the wrist, she opened the door and walked in.

Ben's broad back was to her, the same back her nails had dug into just a few hours ago. She'd clung to him for dear life as he filled her completely and brought her to mind- shattering climaxes over and over again. Violet gave herself a mental slap as she placed her purse on her desk. Ben turned around to face her, a look on his face that was close to indifference. It stunned her a little, but hey! He was keeping the same secret.

"Good morning, Violet," he said with a nod before turning back to his computer screen.

She pressed her lips together briefly before nodding in reply. "G'morning, Ben."

The tension between them was thick, and a fog filled her brain as she struggled to keep from turning around and kissing him right there. The urges that swept through her were overwhelming; she'd forgotten what it was like to be so into someone.

Finally, Ben spoke again. "Violet, is it true that the cameras here in the office aren't equipped with sound?"

She cleared her throat before answering, "Um, yeah. I saw the last manager check the cameras a couple of times."

"Okay, good," he muttered, typing furiously on his keyboard.

She clicked the print icon, having just accepted a stack of orders as a means of keeping herself busy and her eyes off of him. As paper rushed from the printer behind her, she turned toward it as a subtle way of watching Ben out of the corner of her eye. He was bent over his work station, foot tapping out an impatient rhythm as he stared at his screen and typed words into an email window. She stood and collected her print-outs; she thought she heard the squeak of his chair as he wheeled it about. Sure enough, he was staring at her. His eyes had gone dark and mischievous; his stare could have been misconstrued for murderous had she not seen the same expression in his face when they were in the throes of passion.

"Listen, Vi," he said, his voice calm and even. "I think that, for today, you should probably stay on the floor as much as possible."

She gulped. "Why?"

"Because it feels like I haven't heard you moan my name in forever," he replied without expression, "and I'm afraid I won't be able to control my urge to bend you over that desk and have my way with you. Understand?"

She bit her bottom lip to keep from dissolving into a pile of mush. "Loud and clear."

Without a word, she gathered her items and excused herself from the office. She may have decided on the spot that she wasn't going to let Ben see how easily he could turn her on, but that didn't stop her from smiling uncontrollably as she headed through the prep area and onto the sales floor.

Violet decorated cake after cake, unable to get her mind off of Ben. Their chance meeting, impromptu date, and the events that followed certainly seemed like kismet, at least to her romantic soul. Steve absolutely did her a favor by standing her up—in hindsight, she couldn't believe she'd even considered meeting up with him. But her momentary lapse of judgment combined with his typical douchebag behavior had resulted in one hell of an outcome. She couldn't remember ever having a night like that— not even with Steve, the guy she'd once called the

Company Ink

love of her life. She was going to have to be extra careful to avoid dropping a cake today.

She managed to keep herself from dropping anything, but there was nothing she could do about the smile on her face. Eventually, Jay approached her again, this time more determined than ever to get a playful rise out of her.

"I've got it!" he exclaimed. "It was that hot, Tasmanian-devil type that came in to visit you earlier this week."

Violet paused while inscribing a cake, giving Jaya confused look. "What?"

"The guy, the glow. It was him, wasn't it? The guy practically hanging over the glass to talk to you—weren't you guys chatting near the fountain across the street? It looked pretty intense."

Violet rolled her eyes, going back to her work. "It was definitely intense, and not in a good way."

"So who was it? Come on, tell me. No one just comes to work at six in the morning looking that radiant!"

Violet laughed. "Jay, let it go. We've got buttercream to worry about, remember?"

"Aw man, you suck right now, Vi," he said with an air of playful disappointment, traipsing away with a spring in his step. "But you watch, I'll figure it out!"

Violet exhaled deeply, nervous pangs rattling her tummy. *I hope not ...*

∼

ULTIMATELY, she was able to get away with dodging Ben for most of the day until, of course, the time came to do production for the next day. She gathered the stack of advanced orders that had piled up in the corner of her station and headed downstairs. To her surprise, Ben was not in the office at all. She snorted at the slight wave of disappointment that washed over her. As she pulled up the online account manager, her eyes slipped in and out of focus while her brain made her relive every moment from the night before.

The office door opened mid-fantasy, and she pulled herself together. Her body went rigid, and she cleared her throat. She shook the proverbial cobwebs from her head and forced herself back into the here and now, hoping she didn't look too much like a goofball wearing a smile that she could feel stretching from one ear to the other. She kept her face trained on her computer screen, knowing it was Ben by the sound of his footsteps and the smell of his cologne.

His voice was playful. "Good afternoon, Violet."

"Ben," she replied with a nod, a smile tugging hard at the corners of her mouth.

She pressed her lips together, fighting the urge to laugh out loud as he took his seat a few feet away. The sound of the office chair's groans told her that he was positioning himself in front of his own computer. She could've sworn she heard him chuckle.

"What time will you be home?" he asked, his voice deep and quiet.

Violet replied, "I should be home by five." "After-work plans?"

"Just a trip to Michael's."

He paused; she turned and saw his back stiffen. She giggled and went back to her computer screen. "The craft store, you weirdo."

"Yeah, that was weird. I didn't mean to lay *that* at your feet."

She turned and stared at his back for a moment, half amused and half creeped out that they were even having this conversation after a single night. "You mean the whole

Company Ink

my-wife-cheated-on-me-so-now-I-don't-trust-women-in-general thing? Yeah, you don't have to."

He turned toward her, embarrassment etched on his face. "I just came off like a lunatic, didn't I?"

She grinned. "A little bit."

"I'm sorry. I'm not good at this. I've been with one woman in the last seven years, and I just found out that she spent five of them cheating on me. I guess I just got ahead of myself."

"Don't worry," she replied. "I know what it's like to heal and get back in the game. You don't have to do this with me—we've only spent one night together and, like you said last night, I've got no reason to lie."

"Got it."

"Good. Because I think everything that happened last night should definitely happen again."

"I'd be happy to oblige, sweetheart."

There was that mischievous grin of his again. *Mmm, butterflies*. "I should probably, um ... get back to work." Violet turned her chair back toward her desk to finish her day's work. From behind her, Ben chuckled.

"And I'll call you at six," he replied.

∽

AN HOUR AND A HALF LATER, Violet was up the stairs and on her way out of the bakery, giddier than a teenage girl revved up for prom. The faster she could get to Michael's and pick up the piping bags, tips, and cake boards she needed to complete her baking project, the faster she could be on the phone with the guy who was rapidly becoming her new favorite person. Going from strained to delightfully compatible wasn't exactly the change she'd expected, but it was definitely tingle-inducing.

She was about to cross Sixth Avenue and head to the train when she felt a tap on her shoulder. She turned her head to the right and, with one glance, felt the sense of giddiness deflate instantly. Steve was staring back at her, his eyes apologetic.

"Vi, I'm sorry. I got caught up in something and—"

"No, no—it's fine," she interrupted, her voice just loud enough for him to hear. "People get stood up all the time. I'm sure it wasn't rude at all for you to flake out and not even bother calling."

"But my dad needed me to do something for him; I couldn't get out of it."

She shook her head dismissively and crossed the street without another word; her strong legs took lengthy strides, forcing him into a slow jog to keep up with her.

He hopped onto the sidewalk on the other side of the street. "I literally had no choice." Violet stopped suddenly and turned to face him. "Oh, you literally had no choice. Is

your dad sick?"

Steve paused. "Um, no."

"Is he dead?"

Steve's eyebrows knitted together as he gave her a bewildered look. "No!"

"Okay," she said evenly. "Well then, was your phone broken? Were there no working telephone lines in the whole of Co-op City?"

Steve tilted his head to one side. "Okay, Vi. I get it."

"Good. Because humans call other humans to give them the heads up when they can't make it somewhere—you might want to file that away for your next date."

Company Ink

She began walking away again and, much to her disappointment, Steve followed. "Come on, Vi, wait!"

She sucked her teeth and stopped, staring at him expectantly as she impatiently shifted her weight to one hip. His entire body language changed quite suddenly, and she was actually able to see the moment his charming switch flipped to the "on" position. Pre- collegiate Violet would have turned into mush. Even pre-Ben Violet might've melted a little. But this Violet—"Post-Steve, New Man, New Life" Violet? *No way.*

He took a step closer and smiled carefully. "Are you really not going to give me a second chance?"

She raised an eyebrow and sniffed. "No, I'm really not."

"Come on, hun," he replied softly. "We have a history together."

Violet nodded, softening her expression. "You're right, we do have history. One that includes you emptying my bank account, cheating on me, and leaving me without so much as a Post-it. Forgive me if I'm not willing to fall at your feet anymore."

"Sweetie, you can't honestly believe that I'm—"

"It's fine. I don't know what possessed me to make the date with you in the first place because, the truth is, I moved on a long time ago. And, honestly, you standing me up was pretty much the best thing ever."

Steve blinked a few times; she knew he was trying to process what was definitely the strongest statement she'd ever made to him.

Violet retreated, refusing to make a scene as she held her back straight and kept her smile pleasant. "Take care of yourself, Steve."

Steve's eyebrows were back in the knitted position; he clearly couldn't understand what she'd said and the fact that she was backing up in preparation to leave. "But maybe this weekend …?"

"I'm seeing someone else," she replied gleefully. "So, have a safe trip back to the Bronx."

And with that, she walked away; she was about as proud of herself as she'd been when she walked into Wynne's Kitchen with nothing but the determination of a warrior and came out with the job she wasn't entirely qualified for. After all these years, she finally saw Steve for what he was: an opportunist who used people and things for what he needed and moved on when they no longer served a purpose. She didn't know what he wanted with her now, and she didn't care. *Let him find some other doe-eyed, gullible twenty-something to fall for his nonsense. I'm not that girl.*

∽

VIOLET WALKED through her door at 5:45 p.m., her arms laden with bags from Michael's, her favorite place to shop for baking supplies. Her landline was ringing. She let the door slam loudly as she tossed her bags onto the couch before throwing herself into the bedroom and picking up her cordless.

"Hello?"

Ben's voice was sort of awkward but, somehow, still sexy. "I'm sorry. I couldn't wait."

Violet sat on the bed. "I'm so glad you thought of my landline, then. My battery died on the way home."

"So you're saying my impatience is actually well-timed?"

"I'd say it's timed perfectly."

"Good, because I was wondering what you had planned this evening," he replied, a hint of that charming smile apparent in his voice.

Company Ink

"Buttercream. I'm making a cake for a friend who's picking it up the day after tomorrow. I figured getting a head start on the icing might be a good idea."

"Well, I looked at your schedule and noticed you were off tomorrow."

"That's right," she answered. "It's baking day."

"Well, thanks to a last-minute request, I've had to switch days with one of the managers. So, I'm off tomorrow, too. I was wondering, would you like some company?"

"If you can handle me baking in a tank top, apron, and a pair of boy shorts, I would love some company."

"Your choice of uniform concerns me," he replied, invoking a laugh from her. "And I

can't promise I'll be able to keep my hands off of you."

"You've got a one-track mind, mister," she teased.

"Not true. And to prove it, I'd like to pick you up and take you to a movie, maybe have some dinner. Think you can spare a couple of hours tonight around nine?"

"Make it nine thirty and I'm yours," she answered as she organized her stand mixer, butter, and powdered sugar. "This shouldn't take me more than a half hour, and I'll still have time to shower."

Ben was silent for a moment. She waited for him to speak, even pulling the handset back and giving it a "Well?" look before putting it back to her ear.

"Hello?"

"Okay, you're right," Ben admitted. "I have a one-track mind, and let's just leave it at that. I'll pick you up in a couple of hours."

Violet tilted her head back and laughed.

∽

THEY DIDN'T GET out of the movie theater on West Sixty-

Eighth Street and Broadway until just after eleven o' clock. She'd spent the entire movie trying to avoid gasping as Ben consistently snuck kisses and nibbles on her shoulder blade. And she was willing to admit that she'd caused her fair share of trouble: her hand may have accidentally grazed his

semi-erect shaft as she reached for the popcorn, very strategically placed on the other side of his lap.

They held hands as they strolled down Broadway in the direction of Lincoln Center, always gorgeous and serene at that time of night. "Having fun?" he asked.

She nodded. "This was a great idea."

"I can agree with that. And it's a nice night, so we can sit by the fountain and … "

His voice trailed off, taking on an edge of unease. Confused, she looked up to find him staring intently at a spot over her head and across the street. A woman who looked to be shorter than Violet stood on the other side of Broadway, frozen like a deer in headlights as she stared at them; Ben's grip on her own hand slackened. Was she about to be thrown in the middle of a stand-off?

"Is that Elena?"

Ben didn't answer, so she turned to get another look. Sleek, brown waves cascaded around the woman's shoulders in sharp contrast to the ruby-red crop top that clung to her torso. Combine the wildly sexy top with her black, faux-leather, boot-cut low-riders and sky-high heels, and for half a second the entire ensemble left Violet feeling a bit inadequate. She made a point to stand a little straighter —while she might have been bigger in size than the tiny bombshell across the boulevard, she still looked like Wonder Woman come to life. *And I don't have to climb on a stepstool to kiss Ben.*

That last thought produced a smug grin, and it just so

Company Ink

happened that the woman she assumed was Elena caught it. Her eyes widened, and Violet could've sworn lasers were about to shoot out of them.

Ben grabbed her hand. "Let's go."

"What about this girl?" she asked, gesturing in Elena's direction.

His brow furrowed. "What about her? Let's go. I don't want her following us."

Seemingly on cue, little Elena stepped into the crosswalk as if she were heading their way. Elena's eyes remained on Violet the entire time.

"It looks like she might have something she wants to say to me." Frankly, Violet wanted to hear it.

"She's nuts, Vi," Ben replied, stepping into the street with his arm extended. "And I promise you I'll tell you everything if you get in a cab with me right now and walk away."

Violet gave him a semi-shocked expression. "There's more than what you told me last night?"

A red flag waved in her mind's eye. She was already playing with fire by messing around with Ben; contending with a crazy ex-wife didn't make this situation any less complicated. For a brief moment, she wondered if coming out with him tonight was even a good idea.

"I think so." Ben successfully hailed a cab and pulled open the door for her. "Can we please get in a cab and talk about this at my place?"

"You're not worried about her, are you?"

He shifted his weight, the look on his face becoming more urgent as he waved his hand toward the open car door. "Please, Vi."

She tilted her head to one side and eventually sighed. "Okay, fine."

Within another half minute, Ben was in the cab next to

her and giving stern instructions to the driver. Violet looked out the back window as Elena stood on the traffic island in the middle of Broadway staring daggers while the cab sped away.

～

WHEN THEY ARRIVED at Ben's house, his mood had changed entirely. His expression had hardened and his eyes had darkened, though Violet could tell he was trying to keep it together to salvage what was left of the night. She was tempted to leave immediately, not really in the mood for the extra drama; after all, if tonight could be considered anything, it would only be their first date.

She was definitely worried that this situation with Ben, whatever it was turning into, was already becoming too much. Still, a tiny part of her wanted to see if the night could be saved, and she couldn't decide if it was because she was genuinely interested in Ben or if she was just a glutton for punishment.

Violet took slow steps into the condo, taking in its simple and comfortable vibe as Ben locked the door behind them. Ecru-painted walls with navy blue borders in the hallway and living room set a warm feeling in the apartment that, until a night ago, she had thought to be uncharacteristic of Ben. She took a step into the living room, enjoying his modern decorative taste as his couch practically beckoned her to give its overstuffed cushions a try.

"Nice place," she said as she glanced at the black-framed prints on the wall. "It's huge."

Ben just tossed his keys onto the table, a now hopeless expression on his face. His voice flat, he simply said, "Thanks."

Company Ink

"Should I just go?"

"I don't know," he answered. She appreciated his honesty ... sort of. "I don't want to let her ruin the evening, but ... "

"Well, then don't let her ruin the evening. Problem solved."

Finally, Ben smiled. "I owe you a talk, don't I?"

"You don't *owe* me anything."

"You know what I mean," he said. "I just feel like I should at least tell you as much as I can so that you have the option to run screaming if you want."

She kind of already wanted to run screaming. After one night, she believed she could tell where their connection was gravitating, and it bothered her. Ben wasn't some guy she'd met randomly—he was a co-worker, a manager, a boss. She knew last night hadn't happened for any reason other than the fact that their initial attraction was given a chance to heat up, but no one else knew that. Staying involved with him had the potential to destroy her chances with Wynne's Kitchen if anyone found out. But, against her better judgment, a tiny voice inside urged her to move forward.

"Why don't you show me around?" she suggested, wanting to break the tension that had begun to rebuild between them. "Maybe we can have coffee—assuming your ex-wife didn't take that, too?"

Ben laughed and grabbed her hand. "Ah, so you were paying attention when I mentioned that last night. Come on, I'll walk you through."

He led her down a long hallway decorated sparsely with photos of his family that varied in size. Violet was charmed by the love with which he spoke.

"That's my sister and mother," he explained, his long fingers caressing the edges of the frames as he passed. "My dad and I when I graduated ... There's our last family get-together ..."

They came to a cluster of doors at the end of the hallway, and he tapped on the first one to his left, muttering the words "guest room" before opening another door on their immediate right—"bathroom"—and finally pointing at a final door on the left.

"That's my bedroom, and here's the kitchen."

He flipped a light switch and led her into the kitchen that sat at the end of the hall. Now it was time to be jealous. In a city where countertops and cabinet space were about as rare and precious as jade, Ben had apparently hit the jackpot. The spacious kitchen boasted the marble countertops and solid wood cabinets that Violet dreamed of having in her house whenever she perused home improvement catalogs; the appliances were top-of- the-line, and her palms itched at the thought of using them. She would kill for a kitchen like this, especially on nights when she moonlighted as a caterer and found herself elbows-deep in cookie favors or cheesecake pops.

"Amazing," was all she could say.

From behind her, Ben placed his hands on her shoulders. "I'm glad you like it. How about I make coffee and you have a seat at the table?"

She wasn't going to miss this prime opportunity to get her bake on. "In the mood for a treat?"

"What, like cake?"

"Well, if you've got the supplies, I make a killer lemon muffin—then again, you've probably heard that."

She winked at him, and he smiled. "That sounds awesome, actually. Go for it."

Violet began opening cabinet drawers, finding her way around the kitchen as Ben pointed out where he kept his utensils, bowls, and other kitchen staples like flour, sugar,

Company Ink

and baking powder. Yes, she celebrated internally, lemon muffins! Any moment where she could bake was a moment in which she felt right. And she was a little surprised to find that she was excited to share it with him.

She felt Ben's eyes on her as she measured dry ingredients and put them aside. "You bake like this at home?"

"What, like a human? Yeah." *How else am I supposed to bake?*

They laughed, and Ben continued, "I mean, you're setting up mise en place like the bakers would at the bakery."

"It'd be a mess if I did it any other way, silly."

"No, you're right," Ben agreed. "I would have already spilled flour on my pants by now."

She snickered. "And if your icing skills are any indication, you probably would have mixed all this together wrong, baked it at the wrong temperature, and somehow would have pulled wallpaper out of the oven."

He dipped his fingers into the flour canister next to her and flicked a little bit at her with a smile. "Duly noted, smartass."

Violet enjoyed the carefree air that had sprung up between them. "You wanna hand me a mixing bowl, you flour waster?"

Ben reached into the cabinet above his head and grabbed a large silver mixing bowl before pulling open a drawer to his right and producing a whisk. He handed both to her, a charming grin on his face and a playful glint in his deep-set blue eyes. His boyish expression set off fireworks in her tummy, and she felt her cheeks heat up as she took the bowl and whisk from him.

Violet turned away, dumping all the dry ingredients into the large bowl before combining the liquid ingredients. She avoided his gaze as she relished the flirty energy that had sparked with that single moment. "Boy, all these late-night treats. I'm gonna end up rolling myself home."

As she set up the muffin tin by pressing liners into them, she could hear a cabinet open and two mugs clink together. "Oh, you're assuming I'm letting you go home tonight?"

She licked her lips and poured the liquid ingredients into the dry as her tummy jumped. Whisking briskly, she replied, "You know, I normally have an answer for everything. But right now, I just ... I don't."

Ben began to laugh when a noise at the end of the hallway stopped him short. Violet looked in the direction of the door; Ben was already stepping toward the kitchen entrance.

"You're kidding me," he grumbled.

"What is it?"

"Shh," he urged, stepping into the hallway. "Stay here."

Ben disappeared, and she continued to stare into the hallway as she mixed her muffin batter. She first heard footsteps, then the lock of his door as it tumbled open.

"Damn it, I thought you were Elena," he cursed. "I really have to change these locks."

To Violet's surprise, she heard a woman respond. "If you called more, I wouldn't have had to come down here. What's wrong with you, anyway? Wait, did I interrupt something?"

Violet's heart pounded as two pairs of footsteps headed toward the kitchen. She waited with bated breath as Ben re-entered, followed by a slender, darkly dressed girl about her own age.

He pursed his lips, looking slightly embarrassed. "Vi, this is my sister, Lisa."

Chapter Seven

Ben's gaze moved from Violet to Lisa a number of times, hoping that his sister hadn't inadvertently made things uncomfortable by showing up unannounced. So far, thankfully, Violet seemed at ease as she leaned against the doorjamb in the living room entrance.

Tall and crimson-haired, Lisa stood in front of their television, arms crossed over her chest, looking like the cat that ate the canary. And if his little sister didn't wipe that look off her face, he might very well send her back to Bloomfield in a cab.

"Oh, Ben," she cooed. "This is too delicious."

He groaned and ran a hand through his hair. "Could you not make a big deal about this? And when did you dye your hair red?"

"Last week," she answered. "And don't change the subject. When did this happen, you two?"

"Yesterday, actually," Violet replied.

On a laugh, Lisa said, "Oh, wow, so I'm really intruding here! I'm sorry. Mom wanted me to come check on you, and I only got out of class an hour ago."

Ben sighed. "You should have called."

He looked to Violet, who seemed as amused by all of this as Lisa. She was being a real champ about this so far—he made a mental note to make it up to her later.

"It's actually fine," Violet said. "We were just making some late-night coffee and muffins."

"Muffins? Did my brother actually have anything to do with the baking?"

Ben gestured toward Violet, who raised her hand. "Nope, just me. He's on coffee duty; I'm making the good stuff."

"How sweet is that? Oh my God, I feel bad for intruding."

"Don't be silly," Violet said with a smile. "Excuse me a minute, I actually have to get them in the oven if we're going to have any."

Violet disappeared toward the back, and Ben dropped onto the love seat, burying his face in his hands.

"I'm sorry, Ben! How was I supposed to know you're seeing someone else?"

"You would have known if you'd called!"

"Maybe I can still get home—"

"Don't be ridiculous. It's after midnight." *My sister, the drama queen.*

Lisa took a seat on the couch that sat perpendicular to the love seat. "So what's going on with Violet?"

What *was* going on with Violet? It was only day two, so the safe bet would be to say "nothing, really." But between seeing Elena in front of the movie theater and his sister's

impromptu appearance, Violet had just gotten thrown into more of his life than he was ready for her to see. He didn't want to be secretive by any means, but he had hoped to be allowed to roll out the crazy in smaller increments.

Company Ink

"I don't know," he answered. "This wasn't exactly something I planned."

The sound of Violet's voice surprised him. "That's right. We just kind of—happened."

"And he got to tell you about Elena?" Lisa asked.

"A little bit," Violet answered. "We were gonna talk about it some more tonight."

Ben folded his arms and shifted, uncomfortable with his sister and—girlfriend? mistress?—talking about him as if he weren't even in the room.

"She knows the basics," he added. "And I'm guessing you have more to tell me or you wouldn't be here."

Lisa shook her head. "I told you, I came by for Mom. She wanted me to check on you and—come on, Violet, sit down."

Instinctively, Ben casually patted the cushion next to his own and glanced at Violet. *Whoa, that came a little too naturally.* Violet visibly tensed at the same time he did, so

she definitely noticed the "couple-y" gesture. Relief washed over him when she sat down. *Okay, good, she's not freaking out.*

"So is Mom still convinced I'm in trouble?" Violet didn't need to hear that his mother, as of his last conversation with Lisa, had actually used the word "suicidal."

"I've been doing so much damage control with her these days," Lisa replied. "You know how she thinks. Elena's been around for so long. Mom is convinced no one knows you like your wife would."

Ben tilted his head back and ran his hands down his face, wishing he could understand why Elena was going to such great lengths to make the divorce as dirty as possible.

"But she's my mother. How could anyone know me more than she would? Or more than you?"

"That's what I tell her," Lisa continued. "But every

time I think I'm gaining ground, Elena pops up with her sob stories and her bullshit concerns, and Mom's wringing her hands again. Mom wants you to come home."

Ben shook his head quickly. "Not happening. I'm not letting Elena run me out of town like some B-rated Western movie. If she wants to fight the entire way through this divorce, I'll do it. But I won't let her win, and I won't let her lie."

"She's been spending a lot of time in New Jersey," Lisa remarked. "And if I know Elena like I think I do, she's gonna try and subpoena Mom to inadvertently speak against you. I'm sorry, Violet—this has gotta be too much."

Ben looked to Violet, who was chewing her bottom lip with a knitted brow. She looked thoroughly engrossed in what Lisa was saying.

Suddenly, Violet blinked. "Huh? Oh, totally—it's a lot to hear. But everyone's got their battles, I guess. How would Elena even do that?"

"All she needs is for a lawyer to get Mom to admit she's worried about Ben's well-being," Lisa replied. "Mom's been a worrywart all our lives, and Ben's never been an open book, so it would be easy for her to accidentally corroborate Elena's story."

Violet's hand was warm against his knee as she patted it. Tingles started in his stomach, spreading throughout his body. *Not now, dummy.*

"Maybe you should head out to New Jersey yourself." Ben nodded. She was hot *and* right. "Yeah, I know."

"This is what I've been trying to tell you," Lisa said, her voice growing stern. "I can only tell her so much before you have to start speaking for yourself. You and Elena have

been together so long that Mom can't even begin to believe that she's a lunatic."

Company Ink

Violet looked to Lisa. "But you do?"

"From day one."

Ben jerked his head upward, giving his sister a look of disbelief. "Oh, stop it."

"You stop it," Lisa interrupted. "Why do you think I left the wedding early? Why do you think I never came in to visit unless she was away on business trips?"

Ben scoffed. "Business trips."

"That's neither here nor there at this point," Lisa insisted. "She and I have always been on the outs. When you guys first started dating, she let me know in no uncertain terms that she thought our relationship was unnatural because of how close we were."

Violet's bemusement matched Ben's as he replied, "Why didn't you tell me this?"

"Would you have believed me?" Lisa asked, leaning back into the couch. "Would young, starry-eyed Ben have believed his barely-of-age sister when she said the hot hostess wasn't on the up and up?"

"You should have given me the chance to prove you wrong."

Violet looked to Lisa. "You know, she saw us coming out of the movie theater about an hour ago."

"She's on a mission," Lisa said. "And, honestly, I don't know what she's up to—but either way, I've got his back."

Ben shook his head. "I told her I don't need a bodyguard. But here she is."

He expected to hear Violet's laugh in response, but instead she nodded. "I can respect that. Every guy should have a protective sister."

Lisa smiled and looked at Ben as she gestured toward Violet. "I like this one."

WHEN BEN WOKE up the next morning, he was going over his morning routine before he even opened his eyes. He was usually running around from dawn until dusk, even on his day off. But today he liked the idea of staying in and lounging around, and the reason for the change in pace was lying right next to him. The gorgeous woman with the wild curls, impossibly gray sparklers for eyes, and strong but feminine curves lay fast asleep just inches away. He examined her with a content smile, able to see every contour of her face thanks to the scrunchie Violet had borrowed from Lisa to put her hair up before bed. She stretched comfortably in her sleep and turned over, effectively barring Ben from his preferred view. He leaned forward and gave her shoulder blade a careful kiss.

His sister was a fair enough distance away that she wouldn't be disturbed by his stirring, but he took care to avoid waking her anyway. He smiled to himself again—Violet, try as he might to persuade her otherwise, had refused to do any more than kiss him because Lisa was, in her mind, "right down the hall." He'd pointed out the size of the apartment and the fact that a rather large office separated his room from the living room, but Violet would have none of it. So Ben was left holding her, chatting until they fell asleep; he realized, just as his eyelids were about to close, just how long it had been since he'd emotionally connected with anyone. And the thought terrified him.

Violet could have been just like any girl. Hell, she could have been just like Elena. Sure, the last two nights with her had been amazing, but what would she be like in two weeks? Two months? Two years, if he dared think that far ahead? Two years was exactly what it took for Elena to pull away from him. And he still didn't fully understand why. What if, like Elena had been insisting, their divorce really was his fault? What if there was something fundamentally

Company Ink

wrong with him that drove Violet away? His stomach officially in knots, Ben climbed out of bed.

He stepped into the kitchen to call his building maintenance department about changing the locks on his doors when his cell phone rang. He raised an eyebrow at the "private" listing flashing on his screen before throwing caution to the wind and accepting the call.

"Hello?"

"It's Tommy. What were you up to last night?"

"I had a date. Why?"

"Because Elena saw you, that's why."

"I know, I looked her in the face. Did you know she showed up at my house unannounced and said she'd destroy me?"

Tommy paused. "I heard about that, but of course that wasn't how she described it to my source."

"How did she describe it?"

"That she showed up to talk and you verbally assaulted her before physically tossing her out of the condo. And now that she's seen you with someone new, she's looking to prove that you were cheating on her way before you kicked her out."

He turned away from the sink, water blasting out of the faucet and splashing large droplets all over the pristine counter as he took a seat at the dinette. "Kicked her out? She left me!"

"I know, but this is what she's saying," Tommy warned. "Just keep it together, and watch what you do in public. She may have a private eye follow you. And I wouldn't be surprised if she tried to postdate the photos."

"How would she even pull that off?"

"We're in the age of digital photography, my friend. A little Photoshop goes a long way."

Ben remained silent, dropping his head in his hand.

Tommy continued, "I know this is frustrating. She's trying to break you, I know this for a fact. What it comes down to is that you're worth a lot of money if she can angle things right—even more if she can prove abuse or infidelity. And if she can get a judge to see both, you're screwed."

"But none of it's true!" Ben exclaimed. "I spent seven years treating her like a damn princess! Anything she wanted, I gave her. She wanted jewelry, I gave it to her. She wanted a car, I gave it to her. She wanted space, and I gave it to her. What did I get in return? Elena walked out on me with Ethan carrying her full set of Chanel luggage—which I bought her!"

"Bro, I know," Tommy reassured him. "It's a house of cards, I promise you. And the case I'm developing will break her; if I can get this source to come out of the shadows, her entire story will fall apart. You've just got to trust me."

"Is your source credible?"

"Highly."

Ben frowned. "And you're sure they're not playing you?"

Tommy paused. "Like, 97 percent sure."

"You're giving me condom odds on a source that can make or break me?"

"It'll be a 100 percent soon. Just let me do what I do."

"Don't make me regret this."

"Just be careful. And you're gonna have to tell me about this new girl."

"I'll tell you all about her, but you already know who she is."

Tommy only needed to think briefly before laughing. "Whoa, the production supervisor? How? When?"

"Long story," Ben answered.

Company Ink

"I can't wait to hear it. I've gotta run, but I'm going to text you later. Maybe we can have a drink in your neighborhood."

"Yeah, that's a possibility. I'll let you know later."

After the call ended, Ben placed his phone back on the table and spent a long moment staring at it. Most guys fresh out of a marriage and headed toward divorce, especially when they were the ones who got cheated on, had a much longer mourning period than the handful of weeks he'd spent in the Caribbean. Then again, most women weren't like Elena. Even saying her name in his mind set off a wave of anxiety; he couldn't understand why she wouldn't just go away. If she had kept proceedings clean, he might have even paid alimony without so much as a grumble. But the idea that she was after much more than that—that she was out to break him—hurt more than the fact that she'd spent most of their marriage laying with the guy who'd claimed to be his best friend.

He picked up his phone, turning it over and over in his hands as he hoped to God he wasn't wrong about Tommy. The lawyer/drinking buddy and only classmate he'd managed to stay in touch with after college had been the one to reach out to Ben while he lay on the hot sand in the Bahamas, contemplating leaving Elena the condo and moving back in with his parents to start over. Tommy had begun representing Ben without a retainer and kept him in the loop constantly. He appreciated Tommy, more than he could ever express, for lighting a fire under his ass and getting him to come home and fight. But now, for the first time in weeks, he felt a small twinge of doubt where his lawyer and longtime bud was concerned.

Yeah, his guard was up further and, taking Tommy's advice, he'd be careful going forward—with everyone. Besides, he didn't want Violet getting involved in a mess that was only getting uglier. It was on that train of thought that he finally swiped his fingers across the screen of his Galaxy S3 to call maintenance for the lock change.

Glad that he'd at least taken care of one thing today, he returned to his bedroom, planning to wrap his arms around Violet and stay in bed for another few hours. What he found was the glamazon baker sitting up in his California king, his white V-neck undershirt clinging to her killer curves. Her olive-skinned gams were drawn to her chest, and her arms were wrapped around them. She'd taken her hair out of the messy ponytail she'd had sitting at the top of her head, and her unruly raven curls now cascaded down her back and over her shoulders. She gave him a sleepy smile, and he grinned at her sheepishly.

"Our first sleepover." He chuckled.

Violet blushed; she let out a whisper of a giggle and lowered her head onto her knees.

"It was fun," she murmured.

"Would you like some breakfast?" he offered. "I'm a pretty decent cook, but I bet I can bribe my sister into making some of the best French toast you've ever had."

Violet looked up with a grin, stretching her long legs out before turning to let them hang off the bed. "That sounds amazing, but I do have to go. Baking day, remember?"

"That's right, baking day. If you're still up for company, I can be over in a few hours." Violet stood thoughtfully, allowing herself a stretch that revealed enough of her boy shorts to make his heart race. "Are you up for it?"

Ben raised an eyebrow. "What does that mean? Of course I'm up for it."

Violet tilted her head to one side, folding her arms behind her. "Look, I heard some of that phone conversa-

Company Ink

tion. It sounds like Elena's giving you more than you're bargaining for. I mean, changing locks, going through a divorce—it's all trying, and I get it. Are you sure you want to start something new?"

He approached her carefully, wrapping his arms around her waist as he took a deep breath. "Look, Vi, I may be working some things out, but I want to look toward the

future. These last two days have been interesting, and I feel like if we just take things one day at a time, we might be all right."

He searched her expression for traces of doubt. The fear that he was actively destroying any hope of falling in love without realizing it threatened to consume him. "Are you having second thoughts?"

Violet smiled up at him warmly. "No, I'm really not. But my last relationship nearly destroyed me. I like you a lot, Ben, and I would hate for you to end up resenting me for jumping from one relationship to another with no real healing time in between. Even worse, I'd hate to end up being a rebound with all that's happened between us in the last couple of days and ... Oh my God—am I a rebound?"

"No, no," Ben assured her. "I'm too old for rebounds."

And as fast as he wondered if she was having second thoughts, he was hit with his own. His mouth said he was too old for rebounds, but Ben couldn't help but wonder—was that what this was? Could he have been a rebound of sorts for her? He felt like he'd had sufficient time to heal on that quiet expanse of beach in the Bahamas, but was it enough? They were questions he wanted to bring out in the open; he wanted to be straight with her, but he was concerned that blunt honesty would make her walk out faster than you could say *cupcake*.

Violet wrapped her arms around his waist and snuggled into him. "I hope so. I'm sorry you're going through this, Ben."

Without another word, he tucked one finger under her chin, lifting her face to his as he leaned down for a kiss. Violet's heart pounded as her eyes fluttered closed. Their lips had barely touched when there was a knock on the door. Ben let out a frustrated groan and pressed his forehead against Violet's shoulder; she laughed loudly and wrapped her arms around his neck in response.

Lisa's voice was loud and clear from behind the door. "All right, bunnies. I'm going downstairs for breakfast—I'll bring you guys some Gatorade!"

"Get the hell out of here, Lisa!" he called out.

Lisa let out a boisterous laugh, followed by footsteps and the opening and closing of his front door as it echoed down the hallway. That was the cue for Ben to begin sampling Violet's soft flesh with the tip of his tongue. He tightened his grip around her waist, lifting her off the ground and inciting another delighted giggle.

She tried halfheartedly, playfully, to wriggle out of his grasp. "Ben, stop! She *is* coming back, you know."

He lowered her onto the bed gently, his muscles flexing as he positioned himself over her. "If she knows what's good for her, she won't be back for at least a half an hour."

It wasn't long before her legs were once again wrapped around his back, his hips grinding against her as his member filled her again and again, slowly, deeply, perfectly...

~

VIOLET ARRIVED HOME a few hours later, sufficiently full from an amazing breakfast and a little sore from the half hour of bliss in Ben's bedroom. Slow, deep strokes had

Company Ink

given way to a superb pounding, drawing guttural groans she wouldn't soon forget. She sighed softly as she went weak in the knees thinking about Ben turning her over and claiming her doggy style. It had never been that good with anyone.

A nervous energy took over as she left the elevator, walking to her door with a spring in her step. Her door was in her sights when she stopped short, a dreadful sinking feeling sweeping over her as her gaze dropped to the doormat. A bundle of grocery-store roses stood there, balanced against her door. A card was pinned to the floral paper and, without opening it, she knew they weren't from Ben. She looked behind her, a little frightened by the prospect that he might still be in the building. What frightened her more was that she hadn't given him this address.

Carefully, she tugged the card off the paper wrapped around the bouquet. She frowned as she read the card, her fears confirmed as she immediately recognized the untidy scrawl.

I AM sorry for whatever I did and still do love you. I made a lot of mistakes in my life, the biggest when I hurt you. Please call and let me try again. 718-555-2413. xoxo, S.

VIOLET TOOK a steadying breath before picking up the bouquet of flowers and tossing them in the building's trash chute across from the elevator. The card she kept, angrily staring at it as she walked back to her front door. Who did he think he was? She could only deduct that he'd followed her home, and it made her angry and scared at the same time. How many times would she have to say no before he took the hint? Feeling violated, she tore up the card into as many pieces as she could with trembling fingers and dropped it on her welcome mat. If Steve came back, she hoped that would be the first thing he saw.

Trying to continue with the rest of her afternoon as if nothing had happened, she turned her living room stereo on as loud as it would go before heading into the kitchen to begin a few hours of baking. She wasn't going to let Steve get to her. And she really was an idiot for agreeing to have dinner with him in the first place. She'd said yes because she wanted to know why; she wanted answers and an explanation for how he'd treated her. And, truth be told, an apology would have been great. But she never had any intention of letting anything else happen—he obviously thought differently.

She picked up her cordless phone, tempted to call Steve and give him a piece of her mind. But the anxiety that ripped through her as she realized that she'd already opened up a huge can of worms made her stomach turn, so she decided against it. Still clutching the phone, she hightailed it for the bathroom. With tears in her eyes, she bent over the sink and threw up, her phone falling to the floor with a loud clatter as her nerves got the best of her.

The phone rang as she sat on the cold bathroom tile, trying to pull herself together. Violet let out a groan as the caller ID read Ben's name; she wiped her mouth and took a couple of deep breaths before answering.

She did her best to control the tremble in her voice. "Hi there."

"Vi, come back."

She closed her eyes, the playfulness in his voice bringing instant relief. "I can't. I've already got the oven on."

"Oh, all right," he acquiesced with a sincere chuckle. "I'm still coming by, but it's going to be a little later than I planned. I really need to have a chat with Tommy about the

divorce case. Is that okay?"

"Oh, sure," she answered, her eyes shooting open. Damn, that shredded card was still

scattered at her front door, waiting to serve as a clear message of rejection when Steve reappeared in her building again. "In fact, how about we just save you coming over for another day? I don't want you to feel like you have to rush."

"It's not like I'm going into a conference or anything; he's just updating me. I'm also going to—and try not to be too creeped out here—well, I'm telling him about you."

She couldn't help but smile. "About me?"

"Yes. I'm telling him about us, because as my lawyer he needs to know."

Her stomach churned again. "So there's an us?"

"There might be."

Us. The last "us" she was a part of just overstepped social boundaries and left flowers at her door when she'd already made it clear that she was seeing someone else and wanted nothing to do with him. So far, she and Ben had only had a date and a couple of heated trysts; thinking of the two of them as "us" was a lot for Violet to absorb, especially with Steve trying to make a return into her life.

"Vi, are you there?"

"Yeah, I'm here," she answered. She could almost hear the sound of metal walls slamming down around her as she shut him out. "I'm not actually feeling good."

"Oh, that sucks. Feeling gross?"

"Feeling tired," she said, feigning a playful tone. "You wore me out."

"If you're trying to give my ego a boost, you're doing a great job."

"I try," she replied, forcing herself to get to her feet. "All right, hun, I've got eggs to crack."

He sighed. "Get back in my arms soon."

Her eyes closed involuntarily, her body betraying her as it took brief solace in his last statement even though her stomach was sick from the pressure the last few minutes had put on her.

"You bet your ass I will," she replied softly.

After the call ended, Violet glanced at her reflection in the mirror; a little pale thanks to the nervous tummy quake, she knew that if she got rid of Steve once, she could do it again. And Ben, who was already going through his own drama with Elena, didn't have to know. Things were complicated enough between them; he didn't need the drama of another ex. And this time, she was fairly confident she was strong enough to get Steve out of her life on her own.

Chapter Eight

Ella sat on the windowsill in Violet's bedroom the next day with her eyes wide, hanging on to her best friend's every word, the cake Violet had made for her forgotten.

"So you're sure that your mom didn't talk to Steve?"

"She said he hasn't reached out to her at all," Violet said from behind her closet door as she leafed through her clothes. "I mean, why would she lie, especially considering how we broke up in the first place?"

"Well, how did he figure out where you live?"

Violet paused briefly before closing the closet door, a shirt draped over her arm. "I think he followed me home from the bakery."

Ella's jaw dropped as she leaned over and took the shirt. "Oh, no. You don't think he's...?"

"That's exactly what I'm thinking," Violet answered. "And if he's starting again, I don't know what I'm going to do. I can't go through this again."

"I hate to say this, but you kind of started it."

"No, you're right," Violet agreed with a sigh. "I

shouldn't have agreed to have dinner with him in the first place."

"You never did tell me why you had that major brain fart, you know."

Violet chuckled in spite of herself. "Promise you won't get mad or laugh."

Ella was already smiling. "I'm listening, not promising."

"All right, fine. Here's the thing—it's complicated. I know it seems like I did it out of spite, but I wanted to hear him say he was wrong. I wanted to know why he treated me the way he did."

Ella made a noise that sounded like a mixture of a frustrated groan and a laugh. She placed her hands over her face. "And there it is—women and our quest for why. I'm telling you it's going to be the thing that dooms us as a gender."

"I didn't say I had a great reason."

"You're hopeless. Does Ben know what's going on?"

Violet shook her head. "Ben's got enough going on with his ex; he doesn't need my added drama."

"Vi, you've gotta say something, especially if Steve gets out of hand again. It wouldn't be the worst thing in the world to have Ben at your side."

Violet sucked her teeth in frustration. "I'm a big girl, Ella—I can handle my own messes! I don't need a hero."

Ella pinched the bridge of her nose. "This is exactly how you acted last time, and it almost got you hurt. You know, Vi, sometimes it's okay to need somebody."

Violet tilted her head to one side as she considered the point. Yeah, she was quick to go on the defensive when anyone suggested she ask for help. She also knew her current attitude linked directly to the fallout from her time with Steve. And since then, Violet hadn't been in the

Company Ink

market for vulnerability, because she saw what happened to people who put their trust in the wrong people. But the pleading look on Ella's face was enough to at least make her think about it.

∼

LATER THAT NIGHT, hours after managing to make it to bed at a reasonable hour for the first time since Ben had swept her off her feet, her doorbell buzzed. The noise that reverberated through the apartment frightened Violet out of bed as she tried to get her wits about her. She turned full circle in the darkness, disoriented.

"What the … ?"

The buzzer sounded a second time, and her heart pounded wildly. Who the hell could be downstairs trying to get into the building? It was probably a drunken college student looking to aggravate a building full of people just trying to get some rest. So she lay back down and tried to make her racing heart slow enough to get her back into dreamland.

She had just begun to slip into another peaceful slumber when a loud thumping sound yanked her awake. Violet sat straight up in bed, an involuntary gasp escaping her lips as she clasped her hand to her chest. She stared into the darkness, an immediate feeling of dread washing over her as she tried to figure out how much time had passed. She tried to slow her breathing, but couldn't shake the feeling that she was in danger. The thumping noise came again, and this time she was able to pinpoint its location. She stood and walked quietly and carefully out of her bedroom, down the hall, and into the living room as she willed her eyes to adjust to the darkness.

One more time, the series of thumps sounded.

Someone was knocking. She looked into the kitchen at the microwave clock. *Three in the morning!* This time the knock was followed by someone whispering her name.

Violet could've sworn she felt her heart stop. She inched toward the door slowly, trying to avoid even taking a breath. Another light scrape came from the other side; her imagination ran wild as she pictured an insane axe murderer on the other side, picking at the door's lock with his hook hand. Cautiously, she inched to the door and gently lifted the peephole. As her heart threatened to burst straight through her chest, she prayed the unannounced visitor wouldn't see her peeking out.

It was Steve. Violet's body slumped. Frustration and anger bubbled up inside of her—she might have been more prepared to deal with the axe murderer. Her ex was staring at a point somewhere below the peephole, and his eyes were glassy. *Great, and he's drunk.* What was he capable of now that he was three sheets to the wind? He leaned forward and knocked again; she sprang back, managing to avoid making a sound as the peephole slid closed.

She took a few steps backward, away from the entrance, afraid to take her eyes off the door. She allowed herself a silent prayer as she turned toward the back of the apartment, asking her door to just stay solid and shut at least until morning. In her bedroom, she heard her phone buzz against her solid oak end table. Her hair flew as she glanced toward the front door, wildly hoping Steve didn't hear it. Once she reached the safety of her bedroom, she locked the door and extended her arms as she began to feel her way to the bed. Violet considered, just for a moment, calling Ben. Instead, she reached into her nightstand and pulled out a container of pepper spray—just in case. She laid in bed with her eyes closed after that, knowing full well that sleep would not be coming any time soon.

Company Ink

∽

HER EYES WERE BURNING the next day as she struggled to get through her orders. She kept a triple-shot caramel latte below her counter, squatting every few minutes to gulp down some caffeine despite the fact that the health department forbade such behavior. But if she had to choose between falling asleep and accidentally icing a cake pan or getting through her list with a little bit of energy, she'd risk keeping the outlawed latte at her station.

She did her best to keep her eye on the prize: three o'clock, the hour that marked the end of her shift. If she stayed focused, she'd be able to get through the day without doing much more damage beyond yawning like a beast in the front window. As a result, she avoided contact with everyone in the store, barely saying more than a few words to anyone. Ultimately, all of her co-workers avoided her. All of them, that is, except Jay. This guy was really starting to overstay his welcome—she briefly wondered when he'd be headed back to the corporate office for good.

"Hey, Vi! What's going on with you today?"

Violet sighed, the interaction draining valuable energy from her body. "I'm just tired."

"Hmm, losing sleep, huh?" he teased. "Is it the new guy?"

"Jay, I'm really not in the mood. Can we talk about this later?"

He stepped back, slightly offended at the brush off. "Oh, so you're not just tired—you're crabby, too."

"I'm really not meaning to be," Violet replied. "I'm just having a—"

"No, I get it," Jay interrupted, turning away and heading back toward the registers.

"Talk to you later."

Jay's abrupt departure let Violet know in no uncertain terms that she'd offended him. She sighed deeply, silently wishing he would have just let left her alone today. Still being the "new girl" held its disadvantages; Violet had upset the guy who'd not only been ops manager for years but started as a floor supervisor when Wynne's Kitchen first opened at this very store. Jay was definitely well loved by all of the staff and, though Violet had certainly made a few friends, it wouldn't fare well for her that she'd upset the company darling. *Ah, store politics.* Violet hoped this would be the last she'd have to think about it.

～

IT DIDN'T TAKE LONG for Ben to notice that Violet was becoming increasingly distracted and, frankly, it worried him. Since their first "date," he'd craved her in a way that he never had with anyone. Shared shifts at the bakery had become almost unbearable; every timehe so much as looked in her direction, he wanted nothing more than to kiss or touch her. In fact, in the four weeks they'd been dating, however secret their relationship, they'd made love more times than he had in a year with Elena. Now they were going into their second month together, and Violet might be pulling away. Not that he blamed her— secret relationships, he was learning, were exhausting. And if juggling his growing feelings and maintaining a successfully professional rapport at the bakery was difficult for him, then it must be for Violet as well.

Violet was sitting silently at her desk in the bakery's office, going over paperwork with worry etched on her face. He sat just a few feet away, almost feeling the way he had when things were weird between them. Her fingers

Company Ink

sped across her keyboard and, every now and then, she'd stop and put her head down, letting out a sigh.

After ten minutes of debating with himself, he decided he couldn't wait until later to talk to her. "Is everything okay, Vi?"

She jumped slightly, as if she'd barely registered his presence before that moment. "Huh? Oh, yeah. I'm fine."

"Are you sure?" he pressed gently. "You've sighed six times in the last ten minutes. It's not the orders, is it? Am I pushing too hard with taking on more? What's going on?"

"Nothing," she lied. "Really, it's nothing. We can talk about it another time."

Nothing. Right. "You're not telling me something. And I can't shake it out of you because we're at work."

"We've been dating a month, and you already know me too well."

"Promise you'll talk to me when you're ready."

"I will. What's happening with Elena?"

"The fun continues," he answered, pushing his chair back so that it was pressed against the desk. "I'm checking in with Tommy tonight. But hey, you're off tomorrow, aren't you?"

"I am."

"I'm not, but I think I feel myself coming down with something," he said, invoking a small giggle from Violet. "Do you think you might want to meet me at my apartment

tonight?"

"Yes."

He turned back to his computer screen to hide the delight on his face. Her quick response put him at ease; if she were pulling away, there's no way she would have

answered so quickly.

"In fact, why don't you leave me your keys?" she suggested. "I'll make dinner."

"I'll leave them at your station, in one of the icing containers," he replied.

As he stared at the balance sheet in front of him, he scolded himself for being so excited about having Violet in his arms in a few short hours. He was getting ahead of himself, and he knew it. But he had to face it—dinner, a movie, and Violet were all part of a recipe for a pretty amazing evening.

~

VIOLET HAD SEEN Steve sitting on the fountain across from the bakery, watching her as she hailed a cab. Had he been able to catch a cab fast enough to follow her? Not likely. It was that thought that comforted her as she set herself up in Ben's kitchen. The plan was to make one hell of a meal and slip into a food coma, wrapped tightly in her secret boyfriend's arms—that is, assuming they wouldn't spend the rest of the evening screwing their brains out. Hmm, either or, she thought with a smile.

To her surprise, she heard Ben walk in an hour and a half early while she was preparing carrots for roasting.

"I hear you on the cutting board," he said loudly. "Put the knife down; I'm coming in."

She laughed, placing the knife carefully on his solid wood cutting board. Without further warning, she felt herself being spun around. Violet barely had a chance to see the boyish grin on his face before Ben's mouth closed over hers. His touch invoked knee-buckling tingles, and his scent made her deliciously dizzy. Large, strong hands ran down her back and cupped her bottom as his powerful frame towered over her, and she reached up and wrapped

Company Ink

her arms around his neck to pull him closer. In response, he bent down and swept her into his arms. She giggled against his mouth as he held her to him. Ben smiled at her, his eyes blue and bright like the clear Caribbean Sea.

"I love your giggles, Vi," he declared. "This is how I was hoping you'd be when I got here."

"Happy?"

"I know you've been stressed out lately. I just don't know why. Are you ready to talk to me yet?"

She sighed, pausing to kiss him on the cheek. "No."

"Was that affectionate kiss supposed to soften the blow? Or did you want to continue making out like teenagers in the living room?"

She just knew it was a guilty grin spreading across her face. "Um, both?"

His eyes focused on her mouth as he replied, "Hmm, I guess I can deal with that. Would you like a third option?"

"What about dinner?"

"It can wait," he replied. "We can take one of my famous stress-relief showers."

"Famous? How many people actually know about these showers?"

"Oh, you thought I meant worldwide fame? No, I meant fame in my head."

Violet laughed softly as he turned on his heel and began to carry her toward his luxurious bathroom. "So, how exactly does this shower relieve stress?"

"It's a lot easier to just show you," Ben replied, placing her down on the rug. "I'm glad you're already barefoot."

He tugged at her jeans, popping them open with ease. She reached for his button-down shirt, and he gently removed her hands.

"You first," he said with a grin, his voice warm and buttery.

Violet's tummy jumped as he lowered himself to his knees, taking her jeans down with him. Placing her hands on his shoulders, she stepped out of them. He picked them up and tossed them carelessly on top of the dark wicker hamper. He stepped behind her, keeping one hand on her shoulder as he reached into the shower and turned it on. Within seconds, steam started to fill the bathroom. Ben's hands massaged her sore neck. Her eyes fluttered closed as her entire body began to ignite.

"Arms up," he demanded gently.

Violet did as she was told, and Ben lifted her shirt up and over her head. His slender fingers ran teasingly up her spine as he removed her bra, and she drew in a deep breath as little bolts of lightning ran through her body.

"Get in, sweetheart," he said, dragging the shower curtain open for her.

The hot water beating against her body felt like heaven, and the worries that had compounded over the last month began to disappear. It wasn't more than a minute before the shower curtain opened again; her favorite Viking stepped in, his naked body practically making her mouth water.

"Mmm," he growled. "I'm a little surprised this is our first shower. You look absolutely stunning when you're wet."

Violet closed her eyes, not trusting her voice to do anything other than embarrass her. He tilted her chin upward with one crooked finger, kissing her full on the mouth. She was completely naked and vulnerable to his touch. She allowed herself a sigh, and the sound made Ben chuckle softly.

"Relaxed, are we?"

Violet nodded as he positioned her against the wall so that he could get himself wet. She nearly went cross-eyed

Company Ink

as the hot water ran down his wonderfully defined chest, making its way over his rising erection. His skin was perfect, unblemished, and practically singing her name like a siren call. Mesmerized, she reached out and flattened her hands against his chest, running them over his shoulder blades as she wrapped her arms around his neck. They kissed again, and the feel of his slick, naked flesh against her own took her breath away. She let her hands fall to his massive shaft. Once again, he pulled her hands away.

"No, no," he chuckled. "This is about you."

She let out a ragged sigh as he lifted her arms above her head and pinned her to the shower wall. His mouth began a tantalizing assault as it made its way from her neck all the way down her torso. As his tongue blazed a trail down her body, he lowered himself onto his knees in front of her. Tangling her fingers in his hair, she breathlessly urged him on. Nibbling kisses down below her navel led to long, sweeping strokes with his tongue as he buried his face between her legs. She moaned his name as he skillfully used his tongue and magic fingers to make her forget about everything other than the fact that his all-consuming goal, for the moment, had become to tip her over the edge of ecstasy as many times as he could before dinner.

~

AN HOUR LATER, Violet was back in the kitchen, her legs weak from forcing herself to stand while Ben pleased her continuously. Shock waves still rushed from her core to the tips of her fingers. It was with a wicked grin after her first orgasm that he'd looked up and demanded, "I want two more." And with no more than his fingers and mouth, he'd gotten them. He wouldn't allow her to touch him except to hold on to him each time her knees buckled when he refused to move away. She stood over the frying pan, unable to let go of the thought that, when all was said and done, he was due some payback in the form of her mouth on him. Violet heard Ben's footsteps behind her; she smiled as, a moment later, his arms wrapped around her waist.

"There's no way that filet mignon could possibly be as tasty as you are," he murmured, planting a kiss on her shoulder blade.

"Be that as it may, we have to eat."

"Mmm, is that mushroom risotto?"

"It will be." She grinned. "Are we eating in here or in the living room?"

Before he could answer, his cell phone began to ring in the next room. He groaned and excused himself to answer it.

∾

THE SMELL of Violet's sumptuous dinner followed him to the living room. The caller ID told him that Tommy was on the other line; while he was pissed about being disturbed, Ben knew he couldn't ignore any time his lawyer called.

"This better be good, Tommy."

"Are you home?"

"Yeah, but I've got company."

Tommy laughed a little. "The production supervisor?"

"Her name's Violet," Ben corrected, not a huge fan of the way Tommy liked to "bro things down." "And yeah, she's here."

"I need to talk to you."

Ben sighed. "Can't it wait?"

"Not really," he replied. "Meet me at Ollie's, and I promise it won't take long."

"You're killing me." Ben groaned.

"Trust me, you want to hear this," Tommy assured him. "You'll be back up with your lady in no time."

Tommy ended the call, leaving Ben to pull on his sneakers and grab a white v-neck tee that had been folded over his recliner, putting it on as he headed back to the kitchen. A blissfully oblivious Violet danced around, cooking and humming Rosemary Clooney songs. He folded his arms and watched her wiggle her hips as she tossed the risotto in its pan with an expert wrist, the sizzles and pops coming from the stove seeming to match the rhythm of her melodic singing. Putting down the sauté pan, she turned in his direction to reach for a small container of beef stock and stopped short, her cheeks turning crimson as she realized she was busted. She looked at him from beneath her eyelashes and pressed her lips together.

"Um, yeah—that was Rosemary Clooney," she said sheepishly. "My gran used to sing it when she was cooking, too."

"You're adorable."

"Yeah." She grinned, biting her lower lip as she turned back to the stove to add more stock to the risotto. "Going somewhere?"

"I'm gonna run down really quick and grab a bottle of wine," he replied. "Want anything in particular?"

"You're the pro, babe," she replied with a wink. "Surprise me."

He paused to plant a kiss on the back of her head before heading out of the condo toward Ollie's, where he knew Tommy would be waiting. The popular neighborhood bar/restaurant was proving to be a backdrop for some pretty significant moments in Ben's life. He spotted Tommy quickly and took a seat. A Scotch was waiting for him, which he pushed away with a shake of his head. Tommy shrugged and set it next to his own.

"More for me," he said.

"Look, I'm sorry to be short here, but you've got five minutes. Vi doesn't know I'm meeting you."

"I actually want to talk to you about her," Tommy said, taking a generous sip from his glass. "My source tells me that Elena's obsessed. She's itching to know more about your girl so she can use your relationship against you."

"Don't worry about that. I've seen Elena lurking around like some sort of haphazard spy. I won't let her get near Violet."

"What exactly is going on with you and Violet, anyway?"

"We're dating," Ben answered. "I'm moving on. Why? Am I not allowed to do that?"

Tommy sat back, hands up. "I'm not saying you can't move on. I'm saying you should probably make sure Violet is the real deal, because if she isn't, you're better off leaving this girl alone."

Ben raised an eyebrow. "Do you know something I don't?"

Tommy shook his head. "Well, I think I'm close to figuring out the cards in Elena's hand. If I can get my source to go public, we can take her out and you'll be divorced faster than you can imagine. Other than what I can't tell you, you know everything. Think about what I'm saying here, Ben. We don't need additional hurdles. I want to get you through this."

"This is getting really old, dude. You've been hiding this so-called source from me for weeks now; I'm starting to feel like I'm part of some sick reality show where everybody knows what's going on but me."

Tommy nodded, his expression apologetic. "I know.

Company Ink

But if she finds out who's been speaking to me, our case is destroyed. What I can tell you, though, is that for whatever reason, Elena wants to make this messy. And knowing Violet is in the picture is sending her further down the warpath, which is why I'm asking about this girl. You might want to—"

"Elena isn't the goddamned game master in this thing. I like where Vi and I are headed right now, and I'm not gonna let this divorce make me rush to define my relationship with her, period."

"Okay, I get it. Just be careful and tell Violet to watch her back. When am I gonna meet her, anyway?"

"Let's plan for next week," Ben said.

"Give me a call early in the week, and we'll work something out," Tommy agreed, standing up.

Ben stood, and the old friends embraced. "Will do. And thanks, Tommy. Now I've got to manage to get to the liquor store to grab a bottle of wine in the next three and a half minutes."

"Yeah, maybe you should just tell her where you are," Tommy suggested with a grin. "It makes no sense to be serious about a girl if you're already lying to her."

"Good point. But did the king of the bachelors just give me relationship advice?"

Tommy laughed as he hailed a cab. "I'm not a total douchebag, bro. Give me a little credit!"

Ben waited until Tommy caught a cab before running as fast as his legs could carry him to Seventieth and West End. He walked into the wine shop just steps from the corner, planning on picking out a bold red that best reminded him of Violet, who was fast becoming his best girl.

Chapter Nine

After enjoying an amazing dinner by candlelight at the dinette in Ben's oversized kitchen, he and Violet retreated into the living room. He put on a DVD, the title of which he'd never remember, because Violet began her seduction the second he sat down. She thanked him for the shower as she planted tormenting kisses on his neck, sending his eyes into the back of his head when she straddled him in his recliner. His hands were under her shirt, rubbing her back slowly as she kissed him deeply and pretended that she didn't realize she was grinding on him just enough to force his hard-on to threaten to burst through his jeans.

"Aren't we supposed to be watching a movie?" he asked, his heart thumping in his chest.

"Mmm," she murmured in his ear. "We could, but doesn't dessert sound better?"

He took a deep breath, exhaling slowly as he watched her step away from him, her curves hypnotizing him as she lifted the shirt she wore—one of his V-neck undershirts—above the lacy edge of her panties. She then pulled the

Company Ink

shirt over her head, revealing her voluptuous curves. *Beautiful.*

Ben stood and reached for her, lifting her off the ground and bringing her over to the couch, where he carefully laid her beneath him. "Is this payback for the shower?"

"I think so," she said. He reveled in the gasp that followed as he caressed her mound through the fabric of her jeans.

"We'll see about that."

Bending forward, he gently nipped at the velvety soft skin below her navel as he tugged her pants down for the second time that day. His hand reached into her panties as his mouth closed over hers.

"Ben," she sighed, her voice a whimper. "Please."

"Hmm, that's what I wanted to hear. Did you think you were going to get away with driving me crazy without getting a little of it in return?"

Violet reached down and ran her hands over his jeans, now stretching over his erection. He chuckled and grabbed her wrists, pinning her arms above her head with one hand.

"I know, sweetheart," he murmured.

His free hand trailed down her torso, between her breasts and across her belly to the cotton panties that covered her pelvis. Violet watched his hand before looking up at him with a pleading expression. This girl, he sighed to himself. So perfect. She lay perfectly still as he admired every curve of her body. She shivered as he pulled down his boxers before hovering over her again.

"Take me," she whispered.

He held her wrists again, his intention being to drive her mad as he settled his hips between her legs. The only thing stopping him from entering her was the sheer fabric of her panties, and he let that barrier hold true as he continued to kiss her body. He raised goose bumps on her skin with every feathery kiss, and she moaned his name, begging for satisfaction. Once again, he found himself more than happy to oblige.

He used his free hand to push her panties to one side and, all at once, he was inside of her again. She cried out as he filled her thoroughly, her eyes closing as he continued to drive into her deeply. Ben groaned Violet's name as he continued to thrust, his rod pulsing as she used her abs to pull herself up and wrap her arms around his neck. They held on for dear life in that position as they rode each other to an intense climax.

They lay naked on the couch for a while after that, bodies entwined, deliciously sated. Violet's head rested on his chest; he selected a lock of her hair and began to twirl it around his finger while he stared up at the ceiling. If this were his last moment on Earth, he'd know he got it right.

Violet's hand ran lazily over his abs. "You did change the locks, right?"

Ben chuckled. "I did. No more surprises."

As if on cue, there was a scraping at his door. Violet flew off of him like a frightened cat, staring at the door with wide eyes.

"Hey, hey," he said. "We're okay. It's probably just Lisa, and she can't get in anyway."

He pulled on his jeans, tossing his shirt over to Violet as she kept her wary gaze on the door while the scraping noises continued. He couldn't make heads or tails of her overreaction, but he watched bemusedly as she pulled on his v-neck.

"Baby, just go wait in the room," he suggested. "I'll let Lisa in, and then you can tell me what's going on with you right now."

Without a word, she nodded and disappeared from the living room. He stared down the hallway, perplexed by Violet's reaction. She always came off as fearless, impervious. Whatever it was that sent her skittish had to be addressed. But before he could think on it further, he was dragged away from his thoughts by another series of scrapes; he looked through the peephole. As the person on the other side came into focus, he let out a groan and threw open the door.

~

ONLY WHEN VIOLET was safely in Ben's bedroom did she pause to pull on her panties. Heart pounding, she covered her face with her hands. She was more scared than she'd been admitting to herself. This was more than grated nerves—maybe it was time to tell Ben what was going on with Steve. Suddenly, the sound of Ben's angry voice resonated down the hall.

"Jesus, what do you want?"

"We need to talk, Ben."

That female voice definitely wasn't Lisa's. She could only assume that meant it was Elena, so she leaned out of Ben's door to get a better look. All she saw was his strong -back as he faced the door half naked. Was Elena still affected by Ben's amazing body? Violet watched as Ben's head tilted backward in frustration.

"Do we? Because it seems like every time we talk, you want to remind me of why I'm so happy you left."

"You drove me to it, Ben. I had no other choice."

Violet rolled her eyes; she'd already heard enough about Elena to last her a lifetime. Not only had Lisa told her the story of how his ex-wife got wasted at her own wedding and accused Ben of cheating on her, but she'd also heard all about Elena's plans to use his mother's sympathies to assist in her well-laid plans to personally and professionally destroy her ex-husband. Violet stepped back into his bedroom and quickly grabbed the closest thing she could find to a pair of bottoms—Ben's boxers—before stepping back out into the hallway for a better listen.

"I paid for your entire life, Elena. You never had to lift a finger or open your purse. You said I stifled you, so I gave you space. And you thanked me by fucking my best friend. How did I leave you no choice?"

Elena shrieked, "You tried to make me something I wasn't! And when I couldn't be that girl, you tried to beat me into submission. That's why I left you for Ethan."

Violet watched in concern as Ben stepped back in shock. "You're delusional! I never tried to force you to do anything. And if I was so awful, why did you marry me?"

Elena responded quickly, her voice uneven. "I don't have an answer for that. The mind of a battered woman is a strange thing, Ben."

"Is that what you're telling people? Elena, I ... You know, Tommy warned me about the kind of case you would likely try to build, and I didn't think it was possible. You evil, conniving little ... You know what? Get the hell out of here."

Elena's voice turned over; it darkened and held a hint of amusement. "We're done when I say so, Ben. And not a second before."

Violet tilted her head to one side, giving heavy consideration to what she just heard. Elena had gone from distraught to threatening in a matter of seconds. It almost sounded as if she was baiting Ben into saying something she could use later. Violet shook her head and impulsively walked toward the front door. This conversation was going to end *now*.

Company Ink

She placed a gentle hand on Ben's back; he jumped slightly and turned. His face wore an expression of shock mixed with anger, and Violet gave his arm a quick rub as she processed the look on his face. He definitely didn't want her to get involved.

"I'm sorry, Ben. I can't listen to this anymore."

She turned her attention to Elena. She wouldn't mince words, wouldn't engage in a passive-aggressive catfight. Violet stepped in front of Ben, clad in his tee shirt and boxers—a fact that apparently wasn't lost on Elena. The petite brunette's face turned about thirty shades of red.

"Actually, you are done," Violet stated matter-of-factly. "Anything you have to say to Ben from here on in can be said through his attorney."

Elena crossed her arms over her chest. "And are you his attorney, fatty? You're playing it fast and loose with your utility players, aren't you, Ben?"

Violet smiled, absentmindedly running a hand over her flat tummy. *Fatty?* No, she wasn't going to let Elena succeed in bullying her into backing off.

"Let's not play games, Elena. You know who I am." Violet smiled. "And now, if you'll excuse us, we've got plenty of movies to not watch."

From behind her, Ben warned, "Vi, this isn't ... "

Violet turned to meet his worried gaze. "No, Ben. It is. You're allowed to let her know you've got people on your side, despite the fact that she seems to be doing all in her power to turn everyone against you."

Elena's voice came from behind her. "And what do you know about me? What Ben told you? What his sister told you?"

"I know what I see," she replied as she faced Elena again. "And what I see is someone who should cut her losses and let her ex-husband get on with his life."

Elena gasped, her expression indignant. "How dare you—"

"Go away, Elena," Violet said loudly, cutting off the rant. "I don't know why you're doing what you're doing, but it's twisted. Get help."

Violet bumped Ben backward as she began to close the door. In one final attempt to rattle Violet, Elena stuck her foot in the doorway to stop it from closing. "Have you slept with him yet? Because he's really a lousy lay."

Violet narrowed her eyes, smiling as she did so. "Actually, I have, and he's the best I ever had. He probably just wasn't trying with you."

Taken aback, Elena's eyes widened, and she froze just long enough for Violet to slam the door in her face. Less than two seconds passed before Elena started banging on the door, demanding that Violet come out and say that again to her face. Feeling stronger and fiercer than ever, Violet walked away, indifferent, in the direction of Ben's bedroom with him right behind.

"You should call the desk and have her removed," she suggested, crawling into his bed and stretching out. "Then call Tommy. Tell him what happened."

Ben lumbered over to the bed and climbed in next to her, and the knocking stopped less than five minutes after he finished calling the front desk. Violet lay in silence as Ben called Tommy and brought him up to speed.

After ending his last call, Ben leaned back against the headboard, staring out into space for a moment or two before looking down at Violet.

"Maybe we should talk."

Violet clutched the pillow as she laid her head on it. "Yeah, I think we should."

"This isn't going to get any easier before the divorce is finalized," he said flatly. "She's only going to cause more trouble. And now that she knows you're in my life, it's probably going to get worse."

"If you're trying to get me to regret confronting her, it won't work," she said firmly. "She seems to think the entire situation is in her favor, and she couldn't be more wrong."

"I know," he agreed, "but you didn't have to get involved."

"Well, I wanted to. I'm on your side, and she needed to know that."

"She *needed* to know that?"

Violet pursed her lips before acquiescing. "All right, I wanted her to know that. I'll admit I don't know the whole story, but she's got 'bully' written all over her face."

"Vi, what you did … Thank you. I get what you're saying by defending me, especially when I'm in the kind of position that keeps me from being able to defend myself. But this isn't your battle. And that's kind of what I wanted to talk to you about."

Violet's stomach sank. Sure, the task of keeping their relationship a secret was a challenge. And she certainly had reservations about their involvement, dating back to their first night together. But she wasn't ready to give up. "Are you breaking up with me?"

"No," Ben answered quickly, reaching down to trace her jaw with one finger. "I care a lot about you, Vi— enough to give you the opportunity to break up with me."

She watched him intensely; part of her wanted to be offended, to think that he was somehow patronizing her. But she couldn't let go of the belief that he was just being honest with her. No guy she'd dated had ever been man enough to admit to himself—or her, for that matter—that it was going to get worse before it got better. Violet knew he was right; did she want the opportunity he was offering?

"This is not me breaking up with you, or trying to get

you to break up with me, understand? I'm just giving you an out. This situation is going to get worse before it gets

better, and you don't deserve to get yanked into it," he added.

Violet bit her lower lip. "How about you tell me how you feel about us before I answer that question? And I want an honest answer."

"An honest answer," Ben repeated, turning to face her. "Do I want to see where we're going? Yes."

Violet turned over onto her back, taking a deep breath as she stared up at the ceiling. She knew what she wanted to say but couldn't figure out whether or not her answer was truthful or reactive to the situation. Ben leaned over and draped an arm over her, resting his head on her stomach.

"I'm not playing games with you, Vi," he said. "I just want you to know what you're getting into. The out is yours if you want it."

"I don't," she answered. Her response was an acceptable one. She couldn't possibly be any more affected by Elena than she already was by Steve. "I just want to be with you. That's all—no more, no less."

In response, Ben planted a kiss on her tummy. She placed a hand on his head, grabbing a handful of his hair and squeezing before releasing him.

"I thought you were going to punch her in the face when she called you fatty," he remarked with a grin.

"Fatty? Please. I know and love my body. She can't get to me with that playground- bully nonsense."

He ran his hand across her tummy, caressing her well-rounded hip as he pulled her closer to him. "I happen to know and love your body, too."

"Is that right?"

"Yes, ma'am. You've got hips worthy of worship."

Company Ink

Her body shivered in delight as she replied, "Wow, look who's after brownie points!" Ben chuckled, kissing her tummy again before lifting himself up and positioning his body over hers. "You're in for a long night, sweetheart."

∽

VIOLET WAS ICING a red velvet cake while she hummed one of her favorite tunes when Jay approached. Tourists outside the front window were watching the display with awed interest as she deftly spun her cake turntable, swiping mounds of fluffy white icing onto perfect red layers.

"Wow, Vi. You're in a good mood."

Jay's observation gave Violet pause. There was a different tone to his voice. Jay had always been snarky, taking enjoyment in lightheartedly ribbing his co-workers. But this time, Violet couldn't help but notice an edge to his remark—it was a lot less playful, laced with just a tinge of shadiness. And she did her best to ignore it.

"Just feeling good today, Jay. How are you?"

"Never better," he replied with a smile that didn't quite reach his eyes. "What's going on with you? Has that glow ever left your face?"

The laugh that followed could only be described as that of the classic mean-girl type. It reminded her of high school, when a handful of girls in her third-period home ec class decided to try to befriend Violet for the purpose of knocking her down a few pegs. She should not trust this guy at all.

"I'm sure it has," she answered with a neutral smile. How long would she have to stand there until she could end the conversation without starting more drama?

"So, seriously, it's a guy, isn't it?"

Violet wanted to blurt out that it was none of Jay's

business. But anything other than an answer to the question would've given him more fuel.

"Hate to break it to you, hun—it really isn't." Violet ended her statement with a soft chuckle she hoped wouldn't raise Jay's hackles.

He tilted his head to one side, flashing a toothy, know-it-all grin. "Now, come on.

Your boyfriend's been by every day this week; you must be doing something right. Look, he's across the street now."

Violet's head jerked in the direction Jay was pointing. Her eyes strained to pick out individual people among the crowd of tourists walking by on the other side of the street, but she found him: Steve was perched in the very same spot in which they'd sat weeks ago, watching the store. His head was already turned away by the time she looked up, but she recognized the profile. *Is he kidding?* Was he waiting for her to leave? Violet's brow knitted together, and her heart began to pound so hard it made her nauseous. She turned away from the window and began to hastily place the cake she'd just finished icing into a storage container.

"That is not my boyfriend," she muttered through gritted teeth as she struggled to label the container.

Jay glanced back toward Steve. "Well then, who is he? He came in here asking for you yesterday."

Violet let out an involuntary groan, placing the cake below the counter. She grabbed her latte and stood. "Excuse me," she managed to blurt out before hightailing it off the sales floor.

Violet burst into the office feeling like the walls were closing in on her and began gathering her things. She couldn't get through the rest of her day knowing that he was sitting across the street watching. Her anxiety began to get the best of her as she mentally mapped out a route

Company Ink

home that wouldn't include Steve finding or following her. She then slung her backpack over her shoulder and turned to head out of the office, smacking right into Ben. She almost screamed.

"Hey!" he exclaimed. "Where are you going? What's wrong?"

She paused, seized with the desire to tell him everything and ask for help. But she shook her head, holding on to the belief that he not only had enough problems of his own, but that she was a grown woman who could handle this by herself. "I've got a small emergency. I got a ... weird text from my mom."

"Is everything all right?"

"I think so," she replied, pushing past him. "I just have to get out of here. I'm really sorry—I'll see you tomorrow."

She let the door slam behind her.

∾

BEN KNEW something was up with Violet, and he was running out of patience when it came to waiting for her to decide to open up to him. He tried as best he could to let her know he wanted to be there for her, but it didn't seem to help. Her continued silence worried him and, despite the fact that she insisted she didn't want the out he'd offered, he couldn't shake the feeling that she was backing off in a big way.

To top it off, Wynne had finally revealed her plans for Violet. He'd received a phone call the day Violet left early. After being sworn to secrecy, Wynne confessed that she and the corporate team had been working on opening a warehouse location so they could begin shipping their treats throughout the United States. The plan was to have the operation run by a two-person management team, and Violet was already marked to manage the kitchen. Ben couldn't have been happier for her, until Wynne asked him to take Violet under his wing and show her the finer points of management so that Violet could take her place as production manager when the facility was ready. His heart nearly stopped; working together more closely than ever put him and Violet at a greater risk of getting caught.

Had Violet somehow heard about it through the grapevine before Wynne had told him? If she had, and the news of her pending promotion was the reason for her pulling away, then he couldn't really blame her. But that didn't stop the feeling of dread from filling the pit of his stomach as he admitted to himself for the first time that he was worried about losing her.

He sat in his usual booth at Ollie's, one restless knee tapping against the table as he fidgeted, waiting for one of two people to walk in. Violet would be meeting Tommy tonight, and they were both running late, which didn't help Ben's anxiety at all. Beyond Lisa, he hadn't introduced Violet as his girlfriend to anybody. Given the necessary secrecy, it hadn't been something he'd thought much about. But introducing Violet to Tommy seemed to make it real, official even. He ordered a glass of red that Violet had been drinking on their first night together and did his best to remain patient.

Just as the waiter dropped off Violet's merlot, the jingle of the door over the music playing softly made Ben look up, and his heart calmed as her gorgeous face came into view. Clad in skinny jeans, heeled boots, and a cashmere top, she looked like a million bucks in a golden suitcase. He loved when she left her curls cascading down her back and over her shoulders like a lion's mane; it fit her perfectly, symbolizing the strength he saw about her. She grinned

Company Ink

when she spotted him, heading toward the table with a swish in her hips that made him consider calling Tommy to tell him to turn around and go home. Ben stood to greet her, pulling her in for a hug.

"You've never worn those heels before," he remarked. "I like them more than I can express right now."

"Mmm, thanks," she replied, staring down at her legs as she did a slow turn. "I happen to love the way my legs look in these shoes."

Ben grinned, admiring her curves unabashedly as she settled into her seat. "The condo is a hundred feet away. Don't think I won't scoop you up and take you there in less than a minute."

She raised an eyebrow at him flirtatiously. "Don't threaten me with a good time."

He sat slowly, his stomach doing backflips at her sassy response. He nudged the wine glass in her direction. "I heard you like red wine."

"You heard right." Violet accepted the glass, holding it to her lips. "Tommy's running late, so we might just have to spend a little time getting tipsy and eating dumplings."

"I like the sound of that," she answered, leaning toward him. "But before we roll out the dim sum, I was hoping to talk to you about something."

Ben tilted his head in interest. "Am I going to find out what's been bothering you?"

She nodded, taking a deep breath. "It's not fair that I haven't told you yet. You've been so caught up with Elena, I didn't want to bother you with this. But it's getting out of control, and you deserve to know."

"What are we talking about here?" He steeled himself for bad news. *Here we go.*

"Well, do you remember the guy who stood me up last month?"

"Yeah, Steve," he replied quickly.

"That would be him. Well, after you and I started dating—"

The door opened again, grabbing Ben's attention. After staring at it briefly, he raised his arm and motioned. Tommy had arrived and effectively cut their conversation short.

"Tommy, this is my girlfriend Violet."

"It's nice to finally meet you," Tommy said as he motioned for the waiter. "Ben hasn't stopped talking about you."

"Is that right?" Violet shot him an amused glance.

"That's right. That's the point of all this, isn't it? I had to meet the woman who turned my boy's life upside down."

Ben pressed his lips together. "I'm sure that's not all you're here for, Tom."

Tommy laughed in response. "No, it's not. I've actually got some good news, but I'll give you a choice. We can talk strategy first, or … "

In unison, Ben and Violet blurted out, "The good news!"

"Well, that answers any questions I had about the two of you." He grinned. "My source is willing to testify against Elena."

Ben leaned forward, eyes wide. "Are you serious?"

"That's amazing," Violet added exuberantly.

"Who is he?" Ben asked. "How do we know he's for real?"

After a brief pause, Tommy replied cautiously, "I invited him tonight. He should be here any minute, but listen, I don't want you to get how you get."

"What do you mean 'get how I get'? Who's about to walk through that door?"

Tommy looked to Violet and explained, "He's a proud guy, Violet. When that door opens, Ben's gonna either walk out or punch him in the face."

Ben folded his arms. "Would you stop filling her head with nonsense? I may have been a hothead in college, but I'm not that guy anymore."

"We'll see," Tommy said, his eyes focusing on a spot behind Ben's head. "He's coming in now."

Chapter Ten

*B*en felt his blood boil. "Ethan?"

Ethan, Ben's former best friend and Tommy's elusive "source" stopped in his tracks, giving Ben a wary look.

Tommy jumped to his feet and held a hand over Ben's chest. "See, pal? I knew you'd flip. Sit back down and let the man talk."

If there was anything in the world Ben wanted to do, it definitely didn't involve letting this scumbag talk. He remembered with perfect clarity what had happened the last time he saw Ethan.

Ethan had been standing in the hallway, less than a foot from the bedroom door when Ben entered his condo. Seeing his best friend standing there holding a suitcase had confused him; when he entered the bedroom, he'd realized it was stripped of everything that had been in it when he'd left that morning. Elena had then announced she was leaving, and all Ethan could say in accompaniment was, "Sorry, bro."

Ben could've laid Ethan out right there in Ollie's. But

Company Ink

at that moment, both Tommy and Violet were standing in front of him, and Ethan looked prepared to run. "What could this backstabber possibly have to say to me?"

Violet put a hand on Ben's chest. "Why don't you sit down and find out?"

He met Tommy's gaze, whose expression had hardened. Through clenched teeth, Tommy warned, "You're going to ruin everything. Sit. The hell. Down."

Ben looked to Violet, who nodded imploringly before leaning in and placing a kiss on his cheek.

"I don't blame you for getting angry," she whispered. "But listen to what he has to say. There has to be a reason he's ready to testify against Elena."

"I haven't seen him since he took Elena and her things out of the condo. I wasn't ready for this."

"I know," she said, rubbing his back soothingly. "But let Tommy work. This could all be over sooner than you think."

The thought of this whole mess being over and done with appealed to him. And he knew he had to find a way to get past his anger if he was going to finalize his divorce and get Elena out of his life. Begrudgingly, he took a breath and sat down.

Tommy blew out a gust of air and took a seat. Violet and Ethan followed suit, though Ethan sat on the edge of his chair.

Ben pointed a finger at Tommy. "You've got one minute to stop me from making you regret meeting me here, Tommy."

Tommy opened his mouth to speak, but Ethan held out a hand. "I get it, Ben. I screwed up and destroyed our friendship. This isn't a 'bros before hoes' thing, and I'm

not suggesting we be friends again. But she's not playing fair, and this whole situation is getting out of control. I can't let her do this to you, and honestly—I owe you this."

Violet pursed her lips and made a noise that told the table she agreed with that much. Ethan hesitated at first but then held his hand out toward her. "I'm Ethan, by the way.

You must be Violet."

She took his hand and shook it quickly. "I am. I'm guessing Elena told you about me. She and I had a fun little encounter a couple of days ago."

"Oh, yeah," Ethan scoffed. "She still hasn't stopped talking about it. And you're in her crosshairs now, too."

Violet shrugged. "It can't be worse than what I've already been through. Am I supposed to be scared?"

"She's unbalanced, bitter, and hurt. And it's not a good combination," Ethan answered.

Ben gave Violet a curious glance, making a mental note to ask her precisely what she meant by that comment. And he still wasn't convinced this was worth his time. Ethan

already sounded like he was on Elena's side. *No surprise there.*

"Hurt?" he repeated. "She left me! And how do you even know what she's planning? Does she just offer this information up to you?"

"What I know can prove she needs help," Ethan replied. "Since the day she left you, her goal has been to get everything."

Ben rolled his eyes. He was just about done listening to Ethan—this whole meeting was turning into a joke. He shifted in his chair, and Violet placed a hand on his knee. It calmed him enough to decide to stay put another minute or two.

"But explain yourself," she insisted. "What is she after? What does she want? And why is she dragging this out?" It

Company Ink

was a good thing Violet was there with a cool head to ask the good questions. All Ben could think about was slamming Ethan's face into their table and walking away.

"It's a really long story," Ethan answered.

"I've got time," Violet remarked, "and so does he."

Ethan looked to Ben. "I'm telling you now, you're not gonna like what I have to say."

Well, that's nothing new. "Just say what you have to say, man."

"All right, here's the deal. I know that she left you, but when she did, she was hurting. She believes you left her no choice. She was angry that you never heard her—and it took a huge toll."

Ben glanced over at Violet, who looked like she might've felt some sympathy toward his ex-wife. The last thing he expected was to end up looking like the bad guy. "Is there a point to all of this?"

"That," Ethan said. "That's the point. You're not listening. If something doesn't fit in line with your plans, you gloss right over it. You don't even fight, you just act as if it doesn't exist. And it drove her crazy."

Ben thought back, tried to remember an instance of that being true. Within seconds, a memory hit him: Elena, telling him that she wanted more in her life than just housewife duties. Maybe she'd mentioned some sort of class or workshop. He hadn't wanted to fight, so he'd handed over his credit card and told her to do whatever. He frowned. *What the hell was wrong with that?*

"She had no support," Ethan continued. "Just your money. She told me that she felt it when you guys slept together, so she stopped wanting to be near you."

Ouch. He remembered that long phase before the end of their marriage where she wouldn't touch him. She refused to share a bed, wouldn't hug him in greeting, and couldn't handle being in the same room with him for too long. Could Ethan be right? In trying to give Elena everything she wanted, had he forgotten to give her what she needed? He wasn't sure he wanted to hear any more.

"The marriage failing broke her heart, and it made her bitter because she only wanted to be married once, and she blames you for having to leave," Ethan said. "The more time I spent with her, the angrier she got. And she wants payback. I mean, I've got a phone recording of her laughing as she wonders how you'd deal with life after she took everything and you learned the hard way that money didn't make dreams come true."

A wave of nausea ran through Ben's body. Everything Ethan said made sense with the pieces of Elena's frequent rants that he could remember; even the fact that he couldn't recall her words drove Ethan's point home. You jerk, Ben. And if anything could get Violet to throw her hands in the air, this development would be it.

He was surprised to hear Violet speak. "So why now? Are you telling me you care about what happens to Ben after everything?"

"Look, I'll level with you," Ethan replied. "Normally, I'd mind my business. But Ben and I go way back—and I've seen both sides of the story. He's not a total jerk like Elena would like everyone to believe. And she's not exactly well, if you know what I'm saying. She doesn't handle situations the way you or I do. She needs help, and her getting her way isn't going to get it to her."

"She sounds determined," Violet sighed.

Ethan nodded. "She is. And she's not going to stop. She's a woman with a broken heart who has an interesting way of viewing the world. And as a result, she's selfish, co-dependent, and often times delusional. I know I wasn't the best friend to Ben in the end, but I can't let her win this one."

~

ONLY A COUPLE of hours had passed by the time they left Ollie's, but thankfully Ben had finally relaxed enough to hear more of Ethan's desire to testify against Elena—at another bar further downtown, where Ethan worked. Violet politely declined the invitation but stuck around long enough to see them off. She and Ben strolled hand in hand toward the curb as Tommy and Ethan walked ahead to attempt to hail a taxi.

"Do you think he's telling the truth?" she asked.

Ben nodded. "I know he is. Everything he said made sense. And it bothers me. Have I made you feel that way since we started dating?"

Violet thought about it. Complications with their involvement aside, she couldn't think of a time when she didn't feel he was hearing her. With the exception of the secret she was keeping from him now, she'd describe their time together as great.

"No, it's been fine between us. But it does look like you've got some things to re-examine."

"You're right," Ben replied. "And you're sure you don't want to come to Babbo with us?"

"No, I'm just going to head home and process all of this."

Ben squeezed her hand. "Is everything okay?"

"Ultimately, yes. Everything's okay right now," she answered. "But this is a lot, and I've kind of got my own … stuff happening."

Ben stopped her. "Don't think I've forgotten about that. If you come along tonight, we could talk about that too."

Violet shook her head, leaning on his chest. "We'll talk tomorrow. I'll meet you here after work, okay?"

He nodded, reaching into his pocket. "I'm glad you said that. Here … "

He pulled out a set of keys, dangling them in the air. Her heart sped a little, and she wasn't sure she understood why. Was having a copy of his keys truly a "next step" kind of thing, or was she overcome because of the incurable romantic that had just stirred inside of her?

"No more keys in the icing bucket." He grinned. "I figured you might as well just have keys of your own."

Tears sprang to her eyes. She blinked several times as she tried to string a sentence together, realizing with embarrassment that she was about as floored as if he'd proposed marriage. "Ben, I … "

"I hope I'm not moving too fast for you," he added. "It just makes sense for you to have keys. I made these yesterday hoping you'd agree. I'm not overwhelming you, am I?"

Violet nodded with a laugh. "Oh, you absolutely are! But you're right—it makes sense."

She pocketed the keys with a watery grin, and he cupped her face in his hands and placed a sweet kiss on her cheek.

"Do you want me to take you home? I can always meet up with these guys later."

"Ben, please—I'm a big girl, I can make it home without an escort. Go sort all of this out, and I'll see you back here tomorrow."

"Okay, deal. And then we'll talk about you?"

"Absolutely."

They were interrupted by the sound of Tommy calling Ben's name. Ben paused for one more kiss before dashing over to Tommy and Ethan, getting in the cab, and promptly

disappearing down Freedom Place. With a happy smile on her face and a giddy spring in her step, Violet headed in the opposite direction, planning to stop at CVS for a salty snack before taking the bus back home. She paused on the corner of West Seventieth and West End; for a split second, she wanted to take her shiny new keys and go back to Ben's house and surprise him when he got home. But instead she crossed the street, knowing that he needed this night out with the guys and she needed a glass of wine and a bubble bath. Violet had barely reached the opposite side when someone tapped her shoulder.

She hopped onto the curb, a little startled that anyone would be touching her. She turned and came face to face with Steve, who looked like he was barely holding it together.

"Making new friends, Vi?"

She glanced to the left and the right, looking for the quickest exit while refusing to meet his gaze. "That's none of your business."

"I believe it is," he replied. "After all, it was you who led me to believe we were headed somewhere."

"What? No, that's not what happ—"

Steve stepped closer. "You were the one who called me after I left you my number, right?"

"Yes, but I—"

"And you were the one who agreed to have dinner with me, didn't you?"

Violet felt her strength wane. Suddenly, she was the twenty-year-old baby face Steve could talk circles around. "I did, but … "

He began backing her toward the CVS window

display. "Well then, why would you go out with another guy? Do you like lying to me?"

Eyes wide, she struggled to find her voice. "No, I—"

"Are you playing games with me, Vi?"

"No, that's not—"

"It seems like you are." Steve was so close, she could feel his breath on her face.

"Why can't you just tell me?"

With a burst of exasperated energy, Violet shoved him away.

"Would you shut up and let me speak? Yes, I agreed to have dinner with you. And you stood me up, remember? That was just enough to snap me out of my momentary lapse of judgment," she said, determined not to give him a chance to speak. "And I don't know where you thought I was leading you on, because I told you the very next time I saw you that I was seeing someone else and wanted nothing to do with you. Now, if you're looking for someone to double-talk and trick, look somewhere else, because I am not that girl anymore!"

"Look at you," he sneered, grabbing her by the arm. "You may have fooled other people into thinking you're this strong-willed woman with a mind of her own. But here's the thing, princess. The two concepts don't exist where females are concerned. So save it for your punk bitch boyfriend, because I know what you are and where girls like you belong."

A voice rang out in the distance; the doorman from a building several feet away was approaching at a rapid pace.

"You are disgusting!" She yanked her arm away from him, completely horrified to learn that, in the years since they'd broken up, he'd managed to become even more of a pig.

Violet's hand connected with the side of his face so

hard, she was sure his ears were ringing. But he grabbed at her again, this time shoving her into the window just hard enough to get a startled scream out of her. Suddenly, the doorman and another stranger flew at Steve, holding him back as a man and woman clad in CVS-branded polo shirts surrounded Violet to make sure she was okay.

"Right, Vi, you're real strong," Steve called out, taunting her as she climbed into a cab someone hailed for her escape. "I'll see you later, little girl!"

~

SHE WAS STILL SHAKING when she walked through her door twenty minutes later. Tears were now streaming down her face; the fear, humiliation, and anger threatened to make her fall apart at the seams. She kicked off her shoes in the living room, pulling her shirt over her head with frustrated grunts as she made her way to the shower. The thought of calling Ben crossed her mind briefly, but she was too much of a mess to talk to him now.

Violet was naked by the time she reached the bathroom, sniffling and holding back sobs as she ran the shower, setting the temperature as hot as she could take it. She stepped under the torrent of steaming water, wishing she could wash away the last half hour of her life. So many things she should have said, so much she should have done. She'd imagined for years how it would be to stand up to Steve, finally let him know he held no power over her. In her mind, she'd failed—she ran when he stepped the game into high gear. In fact, she'd never felt weaker. Steve could still pull her apart without much effort, and it made the years she'd spent changing her life seem like a waste. If she couldn't stand up to the guy who'd essentially abused her all those years ago, then how the hell was she supposed to be strong anywhere else?

Then there was Ben and the feeling that being in his arms could right everything, and it made her angry. Tears streamed down her face again as she reprimanded herself for wanting to fall into a guy's arms like some damsel in distress. Stubbornly, she shut off the shower—*no more feeling sorry for yourself, Vi!* She wrapped a towel around her body and padded into her bedroom where she towel-dried quickly as small pools of water began to form at her feet by the side of the bed. She turned off the light and got into bed, still naked. What happened tonight would never happen again.

An hour later, Violet woke up to a case of the shakes that she'd never experienced before. Her teeth chattered, and the blanket on her naked skin felt like sandpaper. She jumped up and got dressed, her body stinging with every move she made. Every sign pointed to her having a fever. Dammit, her thermometer was sitting in her medicine cabinet in desperate need of a new battery. She groaned and dropped back onto the bed. Had a phantom cold struck during the hour she'd managed to sleep, or was she having a panic attack? The cold seemed more likely, since she hadn't had a panic attack since … *Right, since Steve.*

Knowing she was in for a long night, she rolled over and grabbed her cell phone. It took one phone call, an apology for calling after ten o'clock, and five minutes of persuasion to get another icer to cover her shift tomorrow. Hopefully, Ben had been paying attention the last time they did production together, because the task would be all his tomorrow. Unwilling to call him and go through an explanation and possibly talking him out of coming over, she left Ben a text message:

Calling out tomorrow, not feeling good. Talk later.

INUNDATED WITH NIGHTMARES, Violet tossed and turned in complete darkness for the first few hours as she listened to her phone buzz on the nightstand. Somewhere between consciousness and dreamland, she thought she might have heard her doorbell. Safe in her cocoon within her tightly locked and barricaded apartment, she snuggled deeply under the covers, muttering curse words in the direction of the front door. She had no idea what time it was when sleep finally took over, but she was thankful her brain had finally given up and pushed current events into her subconscious.

When she awoke, her head felt empty, and her body ached as if she'd been drinking all night. The alarm clock told her it was 10:00 a.m.—unheard of for Violet, who was normally an early bird. She tried to stretch, but it was painful; she knew immediately that she could probably use a few more hours of sleep. Her eyes closed, lids heavy, as she reminded herself that she had no desire to participate in the world today anyway.

Her phone buzzed at that moment. *Crap.* There was still a world out there looking for her. She whimpered from beneath her blankets, reaching out and grabbing her phone. The backlight nearly blinded her as she activated her screen. She squinted as she read her alerts: twenty-six missed calls, three text messages. She released an exhausted sigh. Six of the calls were from Ben, while the other twenty were from a private number.

"Steve," she muttered, her tummy wrenching at the thought of him.

Thankfully, the text messages were all from Ben, and they were all dripping with concern:

Are you okay, Vi? Is everything okay? Vi, please call me.

HER FINGERS MOVED SWIFTLY over the keyboard as she typed her response. She didn't want to talk about anything concerning last night. After carefully choosing her words, she finally hit send:

I'm okay, just sleeping it off. Please give me the day. I promise I'll tell you everything tomorrow. xo

SATISFIED, she turned her phone over and tugged off its back to pop the battery out and set the pieces on her nightstand. Finally, she gave her body what it desperately wanted; she closed her eyes and buried herself under her blankets, sleep mercifully claiming her within a few short minutes.

～

BEN WAS at Violet's station in the bakery, gathering everything he needed to do production, when his phone buzzed in his pocket. He had three employees talking to him at once; he held up a hand to silence all of them. He was more than slightly disappointed when he realized it was a text message.

Company Ink

"Excuse me a minute," he answered distractedly, walking toward the hallway.

Violet's words told him nothing and only stoked his insecurities about the night before. Her last words to him were that she needed to go home to "process all of this"; by the end of the night, she was calling out of work and not answering her phone. Sure, he was panicking. Ben was all but certain at this point that his divorce had finally driven her away. If he could just speak to her now, he knew he could put her mind at ease. The time he'd spent with Ethan and Tommy had been fruitful; there was no longer a doubt in his mind that this would be over soon.

Defying Violet's request for some alone time, he swiped his way into his phone's contact list and dialed her number. His heart sank when it went straight to voicemail—he'd never felt so out of control in his life. He didn't bother leaving a message out of concern that he might say something stupid in the heat of the moment. He didn't want to be needy, or pushy, or controlling. He'd gotten the impression that she'd had enough of that to last her a lifetime, but he couldn't be sure because they hadn't actually spoken about her past much in the wake of his drama. He'd given her a number of outs; all he could do now was hold on to the fact that she hadn't taken them and believe that she was being honest, not only with him, but with herself. He stuffed his phone back into his pocket and told himself to suck it up, hoping that the damage hadn't already been done.

∽

VIOLET SLIPPED in and out of consciousness for the remainder of the day, hearing noises at her door at random points without caring much for who was behind it.

Between naps, she thought of ways to stand up to Steve once and for all. She wanted so desperately to assert her dominance, to prove that she was different and that she'd grown. Steve had taken advantage of her naiveté in the worst possible way, and she needed to prove to herself—just as much as she wanted to prove to him—she wouldn't be anyone's doormat again. Each time she imagined facing him, she'd begin piecing an epic rant together, the kind of speech from which he'd have no choice but to walk away. And each time she'd string a few words together, sleep would take her.

She finally woke up, without the aid of her alarm, at four o' clock the next morning. Full of renewed spirit, Violet jumped out of bed and headed directly for the bathroom. After what she thought was a pretty amazing shower, Violet dried off and began to get dressed, feeling absolutely positive today would be a better day. As she set up her usual breakfast, prepped her lunch, and put her bag together to take to work, it felt great to be engulfed in her usual routine. And by the time she walked out of the apartment, she couldn't wait to get to work and, more importantly, see Ben's face.

She strolled into Wynne's Kitchen at five thirty, her usual arrival time. Counter staff and bakers alike greeted her warmly, asking if she was okay, as she made her way downstairs to the office. When she entered the office, she was surprised to see Ben sitting at his desk. He was hunched over, head in his hands. She regarded him with a tilt of the head, her heart swelling as she realized she'd missed him more than she thought.

"Hey, you," she said softly.

Ben sat up straight and turned, worry etched on his face. "Vi."

"I'm sorry. I shouldn't have shut you out like that."

Company Ink

He shook his head. "I haven't exactly given you reason to think you can come to me. I've been so caught up in the divorce and just keeping away from Elena that I—"

"It's okay," Violet insisted, pressing her back against the office door. "We also didn't exactly start on the most solid ground, did we?"

"No, I guess not," he replied. "I guess we've got a little damage control to do, huh?"

"I wouldn't say damage control." She grinned, pushing off the door and walking to her desk. "But we do have to talk. After work, I'll meet you at your place, cook, and we'll talk all night if you want."

"As much fun as that sounds," he answered as she took her seat, "I feel like we need to hash this out now. At least so I know what I'm headed into tonight."

Violet raised an eyebrow. "I mean, our situation is complicated—I just didn't think it was *that* complicated. What is it you're worried about?"

Pressing his lips together, he stood. "Never mind, you're right—we'll talk at the house tonight. I've gotta get the cash into the drawers anyway."

Violet watched him, bewildered, as he clammed up and went about his business. What was eating at him? With a sigh, she logged in to her computer and began to set up her morning.

∽

BEN HEADED up the stairs with two register drawers in his arms, a little disappointed in himself for giving Violet a passive-aggressive cold shoulder. She was absolutely right to say they'd talk later; how in the hell would they ever get a decent conversation in while they were running The Rock? That said, he was more anxious about their pending conversation than he was willing to let on; he couldn't vouch for her state of mind yesterday, but he'd worried himself into a completely sleepless night wondering whether or not Violet was on the verge of leaving him.

Ben slammed the drawers into their respective registers, feeling like an idiot for being so crazed about something that he had no control over. If she did have second thoughts, could he stop her from going? Probably not. But did he want her to stay? *My God, yes.* It was completely unnatural to be falling for someone else when his divorce papers hadn't even been signed yet, but there it was.

He blew out a gust of air as he made a split decision to avoid Violet as much as he could today, only because he wasn't sure he could control his urge to drag her into one of the walk-in refrigerators and demand they have this conversation now. Ben was used to immediate satisfaction when it came to his curiosity, and the fact that he'd waited even twenty-four hours to discuss the immediate future with his girlfriend was a damned miracle. The impatience coursing through his veins would likely drive him crazy before the morning ended, but for Violet, he'd wait.

~

AFTER ONE OF THE LONGEST, most awkward days she'd ever spent in Ben's presence since they began dating, Violet couldn't wait to get out of the bakery. The only thought that kept her going was that the tension between them would certainly be long gone by the end of this evening. She'd cook, they'd talk, and Ben would finally know the story between her and Steve as well as what the jerk had been up to lately. Violet couldn't wait to get it all out in the open and hopefully end up in Ben's arms at the end of the night.

Company Ink

Thankful she hadn't run into Ben when she entered the office, she grabbed her things and sped out of the bakery before anyone could call her back. She grabbed her cell phone and stopped just outside the store to send Ben a quick text message saying she'd see him tonight, followed by a few x's and o's. Hoping that would be enough to make him smile, she began to walk toward the bus that would take her to Ben's neighborhood. She was startled to find Steve, disheveled and wild-eyed, standing in front of her. She stepped back into a defensive position, determined not to let him send her running.

To her surprise, he held up his hands submissively. "Wait, wait! Relax, I'm not here to start trouble."

She watched him silently, poised to punch him and yell for the police if the situation called for it. Steve kept his hands where she could see them, thank God. "Vi, just ... just take it easy. I'm sorry."

"You're sorry?" Violet repeated, stunned.

"I am. I was an absolute jerk to you last night, and I'm sure it only reminded you of the guy I was in the past."

"The guy you were?" Violet asked. "I think we're way beyond talking about your behavior in the past tense."

"You're right," he replied. "I deserved that. That's why I had to make sure I apologized before ..."

His shoulders were hunched as he closed the distance between them just a little more. "Look, I'm going back to Florida. Here—New York—is not where I'm meant to be, and it's definitely not what I need. You deserve better than how I acted."

She watched him carefully, unsure of how to take his statement. He seemed genuinely apologetic and humble, but she couldn't help but feel like he was holding a proverbial knife behind his back.

"Being up here brought back everything I hated about

myself, things I thought I let go when you left me," he continued. "And when you rejected me, and I saw you with that guy ... well, you know."

Violet's arms dropped to her sides. "Yeah, I know."

He held his hands out in an imploring gesture. "I don't expect you to ever forget the way I treated you, but maybe one day you can forgive me?"

She wanted to tell him off. But there he stood before her, seemingly vulnerable and taking responsibility for his behavior by asking for eventual forgiveness. She looked away and folded her arms before letting out a sigh. "Maybe."

An awkward moment of silence extended between them; Violet was considering just walking away when she felt Steve grab her arms aggressively. Her eyes flew upward to meet his and, before she could exclaim, he crushed his mouth against hers. She struggled against him, but he held on, his strength proving too much for her. Bile rose in her throat, and her stomach churned in the worst way; his slimy tongue made its way into her mouth as he forced himself on her. She jerked her head to one side and screamed against him; she felt him laugh against her before pushing her away with so much force that she almost flew backward into the street.

She gagged momentarily as he wiped his mouth and watched her, his gaze dripping with disdain. "Yeah, that's what I thought you'd taste like—a bitter, deluded bitch."

Violet straightened her back and glared at him before reaching out and shoving him as hard as she could. "Who the hell do you think you are?"

Steve grabbed her again, scolding her like an abusive parent would a child. "Who do you think *you* are? You've got it all under control, huh? I know girls like you think

Company Ink

you're strong and capable of protecting yourselves, but let me tell you something—*look at me!*"

With those last three words, he shook her so hard she felt her brain rattle. "You remember this: if a man wants something from a woman, he'll take it, just like I did right now. You got that? Women aren't strong, do you under—"

Embarrassed, seething with rage, Violet stomped on his foot as hard as she could. He let out a yowl and stepped back. *Women aren't strong, huh?* Before she could change her mind, she closed her fist, pulled back, and aimed for the back of his head as she punched him square in the face. And boy, did he go down like a sack of potatoes. His legs crumpled beneath him as he hit the sidewalk, and she found herself burdened with a sense of righteousness and outrage as she stood over him, screaming.

"I'm not strong? I just knocked you out, didn't I!"

For the second time in as many days, Violet found herself surrounded by people who wanted to help her. Her wrist swelled immediately from the well-placed but poorly executed punch she'd thrown; she cradled it in her arms as a group of tourists remained standing around her to keep her safe as Steve began to come to. And Violet didn't run this time as the police converged on the scene. Steve wasn't getting away with this one, or any one for that matter.

Never again.

Chapter Eleven

It was about midnight when Violet began the trip home from the emergency room. Her cab raced up Broadway at her urging, bringing her home after a few painful hours at Lenox Hill Hospital. The beyond-embarrassing incident with Steve had resulted in numerous x-rays, a cramped neck from dozing off in the waiting room, and a manageable sprain in her wrist. Violet was sent home with a top-of-the-line brace her insurance probably wouldn't pay for and a prescription for Vicodin, as well as a couple of pills to get her started on the ride home. At the halfway point, Violet was officially too stoned to care about the throbbing pain in her freshly turned wrist.

The doctors had instructed her to keep it immobile until her recheck appointment, which was twelve days away. Such instructions were simple enough for the average nine- to-fiver, but this was practically a death sentence for Violet, who used her hands—and her wrists, especially—on a daily basis. She'd have to find icing coverage for at least the next two weeks, stick to paperwork in the office and, in short, put her entire career at

Company Ink

risk for the second time this year. Her heart raced nervously—would she be able to return to her original icing speed when all was said and done? She shuddered at the thought of what Wynne would say when she finally told her.

Worries for another day, she told herself as the cab pulled up in front of her building. After paying the driver and practically tumbling out of the cab, Violet approached her building with a sigh of relief, knowing her bed was just upstairs. She was a little surprised to see Ben waiting for her, his frame tilted casually against the building.

Oh, crap. In the midst of the insanity, she had forgotten she was supposed to be at his house tonight.

Violet approached him quickly, letting out an apologetic groan. "I'm so sorry," she began. "I left work, and everything just—"

"Yeah, everything *just*," he interrupted, an unexpected hardness in his voice. "When were you going to tell me?"

Violet blinked, assuming they were on the same page but still a little startled by his coldness. "Well ... I was going to tell you tonight. Hadn't we agreed to ...?"

Ben rolled his eyes and let out a grunt. "Oh, well that's just great. Christ, Violet, why didn't you just take it?"

Violet took a step back, examining Ben's demeanor. "I'm sorry?"

"The out," Ben explained, his voice growing angrier. "Why didn't you just take it?"

"What are we talking about here?"

"We're talking about you and Steve outside the bakery! When were you going to tell me?"

Violet shook her head confusedly. "Wait, you saw that?"

Ben folded his arms, his tone sarcastic. "Yeah, I saw that."

"Well then, I'm confused," Violet answered, her frustration mounting. "Why are you mad at me?"

Ben let out a sardonic laugh. "Why am I mad at you? Gee, imagine my surprise when I go running after my lady to say goodbye and find her sucking face with the very guy she told me wasn't an issue?"

"That's all you saw? Didn't you see what happened next?"

Ben glared at her. "Oh, was there more? What, did you mount him right there on Sixth Avenue?"

Violet's jaw dropped, and her blood boiled. "Hold up, how old are you? You mean to tell me you saw a guy holding me down, forcing me to kiss him, and you didn't stick around to see what happened next?"

"What I saw was you and your ex locked at the mouth. Why the hell would I stick around to see what's next?"

"Did you even hear what I just said?" There weren't enough painkillers in the world to prepare her to deal with the living bundle of insecurity in front of her. When Ben folded his arms again and looked out toward Broadway, she let out a frustrated groan. "You didn't see anything, you idiot! Because if you'd actually seen everything, you would have known that I was in trouble, which is what I've wanted to tell you for days. Have you even looked at my hand?"

Ben didn't blink. He looked like an overgrown child who was refusing to see past the end of his nose. His stubborn expression was the straw that broke the camel's back. With her good hand, she began fishing through her messenger bag as tears sprang to her eyes.

"You know what, to hell with this," she said, her voice trembling. "You wanna jump to conclusions, fine. But don't come here and try to make me feel guilty about something that didn't happen. And definitely don't show up on my doorstep looking for a fight when you won't even try to hear my side. I'm over all of it, Ben. *All of it.*"

She stomped her foot as she searched frantically through her bag. Finding what she was looking for, she yanked the item out of her bag and threw it at Ben's feet. It hit the ground with a clatter, missing his shoe by a millimeter. "And take your stupid keys."

Violet took long, quick strides into her building, wanting to put as much distance between her and Ben as she possibly could. Fueled by irritation and Vicodin, she unlocked the front door to the building with her good arm and kicked it open like a Spartan warrior to avoid using her sprained wrist. It wasn't until the elevator doors shut safely behind her that she allowed the angry tears to flow freely as she muttered her finest curse words in the direction of both Steve and Ben. If she never saw another man again it would be too soon.

She burst into her apartment, slamming the front door so hard that the doorbell clanged loudly. She pulled her bag off and threw it on the floor, turning the television on now that she was too pissed to sleep. She took a small turn in the center of the living room, a light bulb going off in her head within seconds, and she strode into the kitchen. She didn't normally like eating her feelings but, as she emerged from the kitchen with a pint of her favorite frozen Greek yogurt and a spoon, a Netflix binge and some blueberry FroYo sounded like exactly what the doctor ordered.

She was three spoonfuls and approximately three and a half minutes into her favorite Mel Brooks movie when there was a knock at her door. Her eyes closed involuntarily as she tried to block out the thumping sound behind her; she was fresh out of patience. She turned the television's volume up and indulged in a rather large spoonful. There was another knock a little less than a minute later, this time a little louder and more persistent. Finally, Violet tilted her head back and let out a frustrated yell. She jumped to her feet and headed straight for the hall closet, a step or two away from the front door.

"Damn it, Steve, if you don't go away," she yelled, throwing the closet door open and grabbing an old baseball bat from the back, "I'm not responsible for what I do next!"

A muffled voice came from the other side, saying something she couldn't understand. At this point, it didn't matter; gripping the bat tightly with her good hand, she slammed the closet door shut with a bump of her hip.

"I warned you."

She leaned the bat against the closet door as she unlocked her front door, partially wondering why she was even opening it in the first place while also trying to calculate how much damage she could do to Steve's head before it was no longer considered self-defense. In one swift movement, she yanked the door open and grabbed the bat, having it at the ready faster than she thought herself capable of with a sprained wrist. The guy on the other side of the door held out his hands and yelled for her to wait—he was also way too tall to be Steve. As Ben came into focus, Violet realized with a start how blinded by her own anger and frustration she'd been.

She lowered the bat. "What do you want?"

Ben shoved his hands into his pants, unable to completely wipe away the frightened look on his face as he replied, "I was halfway to my house when I realized it hadn't occurred to me that your hand is heavily bandaged. It also didn't occur to me until then that I'm apparently twelve years old and incapable of having a grown-up conversation. I'm sorry."

His gentle humility started the waterworks again, and

with tears in her eyes, she stepped aside to let him in. Ben quietly walked around her and into the kitchen. He made an ice pack before grabbing her hand and leading her to the couch where he guided her onto the cushion next to him. Violet watched him for a long minute, waiting for him to say something. Her heart sped with anticipation; she didn't want to get into an argument after everything that happened earlier, but she couldn't help feeling like he had one coming.

Her lower lip quivered when he first brought her injured hand to his lips to kiss it, then gingerly applied the ice pack. "Tell me everything."

Violet rubbed her eyes. "As long as we're not going to have a replay of downstairs, because really—"

"No, Vi. We're done with that. Just talk to me. I promise I'm listening."

She sighed. "I would've told you sooner, but I thought I could handle it myself. I didn't want a hero."

"Maybe it doesn't have to be about having a hero. Maybe we're just in it together."

"I like that. I guess I don't really know about that middle ground. The last guy I dated was Steve, and he didn't exactly make things easy."

"Clearly. So how did he end up back in your life?"

"Well, I don't exactly know," she replied thoughtfully, "but he was always good at throwing me off like that. He showed up at The Rock a few days before you and I …happened."

Ben chuckled. "Before we happened. Got it."

"He said he was visiting to apologize and wanted to make it up to me by taking me to dinner," she continued. "I said no at first, but then you and I—well, we argued, and like a jackass, I called him to accept his invite."

"The day you slapped me?"

She closed her eyes, fighting a smile. "That would be it."

"Oh, well, I owe you another apology. I drove you into the guy's arms."

"No, no, it wasn't like that at all. If you remember, we ended up connecting that night.

And I wasn't lying when I told you he blew it. I came to my senses and cut him off. I told him I was seeing someone else and that I wasn't interested. And he just ... kept coming around."

Ben's brow furrowed. "He was following you?"

She nodded. "There were times when he didn't think I saw him, and I'm sure there were times I didn't see him at all. Either way, he always knew exactly where to show up and even managed to figure out my address."

"So that's why I almost got the business end of a Louisville Slugger."

"Yeah," she admitted. "Sorry about that. I should've known there was no way Steve could've been here tonight, since I had him arrested when this happened."

She held up her bandaged wrist for effect, which he immediately took hold of to reapply his homemade ice pack. He watched her with an intense stare, the kind that could force its way into someone's soul.

"I'm here for you, Vi—and I mean that unconditionally. This jerk obviously put you through something, and somehow it made you feel like you had to fight your battles alone. You don't."

Violet lowered her head. She wanted so much to believe that it was okay to rely on Ben. She felt him place his forefinger under her chin and tilt her face toward his.

"Babe, listen to me. They're not all Steve. I'm not Steve. I realize I haven't exactly proved that tonight, but ... I made Elena what she is because I was too stupid to pay

Company Ink

attention; I didn't see her. I can't be that guy with you. I won't."

"You didn't make her who she is," Violet said, placing her hand on his thigh. "She could've chosen to not try to ruin your life and instead deal with her broken heart like a human being. She could've handled it differently."

Bingo. There's my revelation. "Which is exactly what I could've done."

"Hmm, did we just have breakthroughs at the same time?"

Violet nodded slowly. "I think we did."

"Come on, sweetheart," he murmured, his voice velvety as he stood. "Let's go lie down."

With a sleepy smile she followed Ben down the hallway to her bedroom. Now that the weight of the discussion with Ben was off of her shoulders, Violet could already feel her body beginning to relax. Aside from feeling a little foolish for not telling him sooner, it had gone better than she'd expected. They entered the bedroom, Ben closing the door behind them. She kicked off her shoes and gave the pajamas folded on her bed a look of longing—she'd never been more ready for sleep. The painkillers were beginning to wear off; her wrist throbbed as she struggled to keep it steady while trying to undress. She managed to get the button and zipper of her jeans undone, but when she grasped at her jeans to pull them down, she was met with a sharp pain that made her teeth chatter.

"Vi, let me ..."

She looked up at him, her brow knitted as a result of the pain that shot through her wrist. With an affectionate smile, Ben sunk to his knees in front of her. He carefully pulled down her pants, offering his shoulder as a place for her to hold. She stepped out of her jeans, and he rose to his feet again. She inhaled his scent, her head swimming as he pulled her shirt up and over her head. Clad in her bra and panties, she took another deep breath, vulnerable before him.

"I'm sure I'll never know exactly what he did to you," Ben said. "But I hope you can find balance with me. I'm here for you just as much as you are for me."

"I know," she replied as he turned to grab her nightshirt. "I won't make the mistake again. Steve and I were a whirlwind that flew right into the trash heap. He all but physically abused me and left me with this need to be able to protect myself. My goal since him has always been to power through, to be a warrior. And I've been fine, honestly. But he came back, and it got out of hand, just like it did last time. I was worried about losing control again."

Ben helped her with the nightshirt, pausing to kiss her forehead as she smoothed the shirt along her waist. "Well, sweetheart, I think you did an amazing job of being a warrior. Except that maybe we should teach you a better way to throw a punch."

They chuckled, and she stepped in to wrap her arms around his waist. He enfolded her in his warm and strong embrace.

Violet looked upward, her chin resting on his solid chest. "We'll have to wait until my wrist is better, but I guess you're right."

Ben pursed his lips. "Why do you think he came back?"

"He played the same games with me that he did with every girl. But in the end, I left him."

He stepped back, pulling off his shirt. "I thought you said he took all your money and left you?"

Momentarily blinded by his impossibly stunning chest, she blinked before answering,

Company Ink

"He did. But something I've never told you—or anybody, really—was that I initially took him back."

"Really? But why would you ... ?"

Violet shook her head as she gingerly climbed into bed. "I really don't have an answer for that. I guess I'd loved him for so long that I felt I had to stick by him. Maybe he just knew how to manipulate me."

"How did you end up leaving him?"

"Well, I may have gone back, but my eyes were open and I didn't even realize it. I started to see his real view of women in general. He was sexist, misogynistic, and completely selfish and disrespectful. I couldn't understand how he could be so cruel, but then it occurred to me that I was encouraging it."

"I'm pretty sure his emotional malfunctions have nothing to do with you." Ben frowned, climbing into bed next to her.

Violet sat cross-legged as she faced him, becoming more comfortable now that her story was finally coming out. "That's not what I mean. I'm just saying that I never stood up for myself enough, and it let him know that he could get away with it. But whatever control he had over me broke after we got back together. So I started acting colder toward him, almost wishing he would walk out again."

"Why didn't you just break up with him?"

"I couldn't get rid of him. He was everywhere I was, clinging to me. He tricked my family into thinking he was some reformed gentleman, but the truth was he was trying to separate me from my family on the sneak. And the thing was, I saw it."

Ben leaned back and placed his hands behind his head. "What finally made you leave?"

"Well, one day I told him I wanted to go to culinary

school, that I wanted to honor all of the things that my grandmother left me. And he told me my dreams were selfish, that I was an awful person for wanting something that wasn't cohesive with the plans he had for us."

Ben's eyes widened in response. "What exactly were his plans?"

"I had no intention of sticking around and finding out," she said, her voice hardening.

"The day I decided to leave him, I gave him no room to follow me anywhere. I went to work as usual and then went to my mother's house. I told her everything that night. She wouldn't let him come around."

"I'm surprised he didn't get violent," Ben commented.

"I'm pretty sure he was afraid of my mother. What I love about her the most is that when her kids are in danger, she turns into an absolute lioness."

Ben smiled. "I can respect that. So was that it? You broke up with him from your mother's house, and he took off?"

"Actually, it turned into a three-day standoff. He locked himself in my apartment—the one he wasn't paying rent for—and tore the place up. Used every dish in the kitchen cabinets, destroyed my linens, and set up a rope from the ceiling so that I would think he'd tried to hang himself."

"Jesus, that's unbalanced! How did you end up getting back into your place?"

"My mom." Violet smiled. "She called him and left a voicemail saying she was on her way over with my police officer cousins and a bat. And if he wasn't gone, she was going to make sure he'd be leaving my second-floor apartment through a window instead of the door."

Ben laughed. "Fabulous. So I'm guessing he was gone when she got there."

Company Ink

"He was."

"So, you think he's obsessed with you because you left? Like, despite everything, you were still the one that got away?"

Violet nodded. "That's what I think. We didn't get to end things on his terms, so he's trying to weasel his way back in. Whether it's just to destroy my spirit or because somewhere deep down he still has feelings for me, I don't know."

Ben raised an eyebrow.

"I told you—that ship sailed a long time ago. I won't let him back in," she said.

Ben nodded, reaching over with a proud grin and pulling her against him for a cuddle.

"He couldn't handle you now anyway, Vi. And now we're going to get a decent night's rest, and I'm going to figure out a way to gloss over the fact that Wynne's star protégé is going to be out of commission for the next few weeks."

Violet let out a sigh. "She's going to flip."

He chuckled. "Rest, sweetheart. I have to work in the morning, but I'll be back and we'll spend the evening making love and figuring out how to get on with the rest of our lives."

Violet snuggled against Ben's chest as he reached over and turned off the light. "Perfect."

∽

BEN LEFT for his usual early-morning shift at five fifteen, promising she'd hear from him before noon. She knew she would be hearing from Wynne sooner than that; Ben planned on sending Wynne an email within an hour of arriving at The Rock. Violet tried to go back to sleep after she'd sent Ben off with a long kiss and locked the door behind him, but her nerves took over before she could lie back down. Instead, she fixed herself breakfast and sat at her dining table, awaiting the inevitable backlash, while the television played hits from the '80s.

Time passed more slowly than a turtle making its way to shore, but her phone finally rang at nine thirty. Wynne's name flashed on the screen; Violet took a deep breath before picking it up.

"Hello?"

Wynne's voice was a number of things, but pissed off didn't seem like one of them.

"Hey, Violet, is everything okay?"

Violet picked up on the sympathy and figured it was safe to exhale. "Honestly, I've been better."

"Why didn't you tell me something was going on with you?" Wynne asked gently.

"We could have handled this in a manner that might not have taken you out for almost a month."

"I'm so sorry, Wynne. I really am. The situation got out of control, and I was already embarrassed, and—"

"You have no reason to be embarrassed," she interrupted. "I'm sorry you're hurt, but I'm glad you defended yourself."

Violet sighed. "Did I ruin everything, Wynne? Is my future at the bakery in jeopardy?"

Wynne remained silent long enough to make Violet's heart threaten to burst through her chest. "No, Vi, it's not. You're talented, bright, and headed places. I want you to head places with my company. Just do us a favor and think next time, okay? You were right in front of the store, you could have called out to someone or even run inside."

Violet rolled her eyes. The ideas people have when

Company Ink

they're not in the middle of a heated situation are all fine and well until it comes time to react. "I'm not planning on having this happen again. And I am sorry."

"It's okay, Vi—really. I'm truly glad you're okay," Wynne replied. "And I'm sorry to seem like I was scolding you. I just wanted to check in and see how my girl is actually doing."

Smiling, Violet replied, "Thanks. Are you at the bakery now?"

"No, but I'm heading over there in a few minutes. I thought it might be a good idea to stand by the new guy and make sure he has everything covered. Which reminds me, I hear things are going uncommonly well between you two. No more head-butting?"

The words Wynne used were unsettling. Violet went from relaxed to on high alert in a matter of seconds. "Yeah, we came to an understanding."

"Well, that's good," Wynne answered. "Because you know I have big plans for you, and his management experience is something I'd like you to observe. Are you sure there's nothing else I should know?"

Violet's heart pounded in her ears; she said a silent prayer that Wynne wasn't actually trying to bait her into giving something away. "Nothing I can think of."

"Okay," Wynne said, her voice going up half an octave. "You know you can talk to me if you need to."

"I know," she replied. *Get off the phone, Vi ... now.* "Listen, Wynne, I have a few phone calls to make, including the police, so I can begin the process of getting an order of protection. I'll check in with you later?"

"Please do," Wynne said, her voice sounding just sweet enough to make Violet nervous. "Give me a call if you need anything, and when you're ready to come back, just let me know."

"I will, Wynne. And thanks again."

Thankful that the call had at least ended on a pleasant note, Violet tried to mark the conversation as a victory, because Steve hadn't managed to ruin her life completely. And though she now needed to focus on healing and getting him out of her life—again—once and for all, the thought that Wynne was growing suspicious about her relationship with Ben weighed heavily on her mind. It seemed likely that Violet would have to make a choice soon; she'd so hoped she wouldn't have to. She already felt like a jerk for rushing Wynne off the phone, but she couldn't risk incriminating herself. And she did actually have to make a call, that wasn't a lie: the routine, having never left her mind from so many years ago, felt like old hat. The next call she made was to the precinct where Steve was currently awaiting his release.

~

BEN'S WORK day was absolutely wild without Violet handling production. She was certainly the most capable member of the staff, hands down, and he could say with confidence that his opinion was not biased. He'd gotten to see just why Wynne had such big plans for her. And now that she'd been taken out of the equation for a few days, he felt her absence big time.

He approached Violet's apartment door, his feet leaden. He stopped directly in front, allowing himself a stretch before remembering just who it was he was coming home to. His exhaustion beginning to wane, he smiled broadly and opened the door with the spare set of keys Violet had given him the night before.

He spotted Violet directly ahead of him sitting at the table in the small area portioned off for dining space. She

Company Ink

turned to look at him as the door closed, her face filled with worry.

"What happened?" Ben asked, approaching her quickly and pulling her to her feet for a hug.

"I called the cops earlier to get my case number so I can get the order of protection, and he's already out."

He was stunned. "They released him? That can't be right."

"That's what I said. He was supposed to have a record, because I went through this with him already," she added, her voice trembling. "And I can't get to court until tomorrow."

"It's okay, I'll go with you," Ben said. "I'm off tomorrow—I'll stay here, and we'll head downtown together."

She sighed in frustration. "I feel like a child right now. I shouldn't be this anxious about all of this."

Ben beckoned her over to the couch by patting the seat next to him. "A little anxiety is natural; he's already put you through enough. Come on, sit down and let me tell you how nothing is the same without you at the bakery."

He smiled coyly as she settled next to him on the couch.

"Should we be having this conversation around a pizza?"

"This is definitely a pizza conversation." Ben pulled his phone from his pocket. "You make the iced tea; I'll order the noms."

Violet chuckled and stood, but he wrapped his arms around her waist and pulled her back. She fell onto his lap with a startled squeak. Before she could say a word, his mouth was pressed against hers; she wrapped her arms around his neck as he ran his hands up her back, drawing her closer as he tried to express just how much he'd missed her over the past couple of days in one sweet kiss.

"You sure know how to sweep a girl off her feet!"

He planted a playful kiss on her shoulder blade, inhaling deeply. "You haven't been to the bakery in over twenty-four hours. How do you still smell like cupcakes?"

"When you've been baking as long as I have, I guess it becomes part of your DNA.

Maybe the pizza will change that."

"It better not," he teased.

He had just put his phone to his ear when the doorbell rang. Violet's head jerked toward the door; Ben stiffened and stood to put an arm around her, staring at the door.

"Let him in," he said. "Steve and I are going to have a talk."

"Maybe we should just call the cops, or let him think I'm not here."

"Don't be ridiculous," he remarked, stepping toward the door. "Steve just needs to talk to someone who speaks his language."

The doorbell sounded again. "Ben, please … "

"Sweetheart, let him in," Ben instructed, his voice even and frighteningly calm, even to him. "If I answer the intercom, he's going to run, and I just feel like we need to try something new."

The intercom buzzed again, the sound lasting longer this time. Finally, Violet stepped up to the intercom and pressed the talk button.

Her voice trembled slightly. "Who is it?"

"You know who it is. Let me up."

"Just let me take care of this," Ben repeated.

Violet shook her head. "I don't want to confront him again unless it's in court. Please don't …"

He stepped in front of her and pressed the "open" button on the intercom box, pulling

her away from the door. "You don't have to speak to him at all."

Within a couple of minutes, there was a hard, obnoxious knock on the door. "Let me in, Vi!"

Ben opened the door and came face to face with Steve. But however startled Vi's ex may have been, it didn't stop him from oozing arrogance and machismo. "I need to speak to Violet."

Ben's eyes narrowed as he looked down at Steve with a slow, sardonic smile. "You've said all you need to say to her. Now you're gonna talk to me."

Chapter Twelve

The longer Violet watched, the harder her head pounded in time to the thumping in her chest. She was in full view of the front door, and Steve could've addressed her directly at any point, but the standoff between the two guys kept both preoccupied. Part of her thought the air might explode, while another part of her couldn't help but scoff inwardly at the testosterone-inspired display in front of her.

Steve straightened his back, as if trying to bring himself to Ben's height. "Oh, so you're her little boyfriend?"

She knew that brand of baiting. Steve's first line of defense would be to mentally unglue Ben before going in for the kill and somehow turning the entire situation on him. But, to Violet's relief, it didn't look like Ben was biting.

He chuckled. "If that's what gets you through the next ten minutes, Steve, then fine."

"What's that supposed to mean?" Steve crossed his

Company Ink

arms over his chest, puffing it out as he did so. Violet rolled her eyes.

"It means you have less than ten minutes to say what you have to say and leave our lives for good," Ben replied, a deviant twinkle in his eye. "Now, what was so important that you left central booking and headed straight here?"

Steve's brow furrowed. "That's for me and Violet to discuss."

Violet took a step back at the look of twisted determination that flashed in Steve's eyes. For a brief moment, she felt helpless; he was never going to leave her alone. She'd never be able to get on with her life, and he'd never let her be happy. The possibility, however dramatic, made Violet's heart sit heavy in her chest. Tears sprang to her eyes; she wiped them away angrily. Steve must have sensed her moment of vulnerability, because he attempted to push past Ben to get into the apartment. Her breath caught in her throat as, with little effort, Ben stepped in front of Steve and nudged him right back into the hallway. Steve's face turned bright red at the rebuff, his anger mounting as he continued to glare at Ben.

"Get out of my way," he snarled. "She has a lesson to learn"—he looked over at her with a threatening scowl—"and she knows it."

The hairs on her neck stood on end. She'd never seen Steve look this hateful before; given the fact that she had to have him arrested no more than a day and a half ago, that was saying something. She opened her mouth to speak, but Ben stepped forward.

"All right, I changed my mind," he said. "Your time is up. Maybe you should think about heading out before someone calls the cops."

Before someone calls the cops? Violet had already taken her phone out of her pocket and begun dialing 9-1-

1. She moved back into the living room, hoping Steve wouldn't hear her and flip out. Violet glanced upward as she cupped her hand over her mouth and the phone's speaker in preparation for the emergency operator. Ben and Steve were standing closer now, and it seemed a fistfight was imminent.

"Don't touch me, friend," Steve practically snarled as Ben's hand hovered over his chest.

"First, I'm not your friend," Ben replied. "Second, I'm not touching you. I'm letting you know it's time to leave."

Steve defiantly stepped into Ben's space, his chest hitting Ben's outstretched hand. "I'll decide when it's time to leave!"

Ben nudged Steve backward in response, and the air between them ignited. Violet was mid-sentence with the emergency operator when she spotted Steve's right hand forming a fist as he drew his arm back. "Steve, don't!"

Ben easily blocked Steve's punch, yanking his arm down to his side. Acting defensively, he spun Steve around to face the door. And, in a final move that Violet almost laughed at, he lifted one strong leg and kicked Steve square in the ass. Steve gave a violent jerk forward, stumbling into the hallway and slamming into the wall before falling to the tile in a heap. Ben grinned as Steve looked up, stunned.

"Again, time's up," Ben said. "If I see you here again, my foot will be going *in*. Understand?"

With that, Ben slammed the door shut.

Violet hung up. "The cops are on their way."

"Hopefully they'll snatch him up before he runs."

"If they don't, I've got his mother's address," she replied.

From the other side of the door, Steve began kicking. The door shook with every slam of his boot. Ben walked up to the door and banged on it with a closed fist.

Company Ink

"The cops are on the way," he called out. "So, by all means, keep denting the door so we have more to put in the police report."

Steve kicked the door three more times before yelling something inaudible and ceasing completely.

"Thank you," she muttered. "I wouldn't have been able to control him. I'm glad you're here."

Ben approached and wrapped his arms around her waist, pulling her close. "Did it hurt that much?"

Violet shook her head. "I'm just not used to needing help."

"Don't think of it that way," he replied, kissing her forehead. "Think back to how you shut down Elena. This was no different—I just owed you one."

∽

IT TOOK ten days for life to finally begin to calm down. She got her order for protection effortlessly; not only was Steve headed back to Florida with his tail between his legs, but his mother went out of her way to call Violet to apologize for her son's behavior.

Violet was sitting in the office, handling her usual afternoon production, when Ben burst into the room with a giddy grin and a spring in his step and tossed his bag onto his desk.

"Are you looking for me to ask why you're so happy?" Violet stopped typing and spun in her chair.

Ben smiled. "You don't have to ask, I'm just going to show you. Check this out ... "

He reached into his messenger bag and pulled out a thick manila envelope, tossing it onto her desk.

"Is this what I think it is?"

Ben nodded. "Elena finally signed the damn papers. She walks away with nothing. I'm free."

"I can't even react big enough," Violet said. "I'd jump into your arms, but, well … "

"Right, the cameras." Ben laughed. "I can't even believe it. I never thought I'd be so happy to say this—I'm divorced!"

"Congratulations! This is actually the best news I've heard all day. I'm really happy you stuck it out instead of just giving her what she wanted."

Ben dropped into his chair, heaving a sigh of relief. "You know how close I was. Tommy really came through."

"He really did," she agreed. "Let's not forget the wild card in all of this: Ethan's unexpected testimony. That must've blown Elena's mind."

"I'm sure she loved it." Ben grinned, running a hand through his hair. "She must've figured she had all the control, and he completely turned on her."

Violet shrugged. "She was her own undoing, in the end. So, are you going to celebrate with the boys tonight?"

"Actually, I thought you and I might celebrate at my place tonight," Ben replied, his voice darkening playfully. "I was hoping to start my weekend off by not sleeping at all."

Violet's eyes fluttered closed. A cozy bed, Netflix, and Ben nestled naked between her thighs—could it be any better than that? "I'd be crazy to say no, wouldn't I?"

"That's up to you. I'm just saying I'd rather be inside of you than drinking with my buddies in—"

The door to the office opened. Ben froze mid-sentence, his mouth left slightly agape as Violet's heart threatened to stop. They were facing each other, but both turned to the office's entrance like they'd just been caught. Jay walked in with a bright smile that immediately dimmed when he caught what must have been guilty expressions on their faces.

His eyes moved from Ben to Violet, his expression both amused and suspicious. "What did I just walk in on?"

Violet blinked, shaking her head. "Oh! Uh, I was talking to him about a variation I made to the cranberry apple muffins last night. I was thinking of bringing it to Wynne."

"Well, aren't we industrious," Jay replied, his smile returning as he took a seat next to Violet. He nodded to the manila envelope on her keyboard. "Is that the recipe?"

She swept it up quickly and shoved it into her backpack. "No, no. That's the—the order of protection. Court docs, you know."

"Oh, right. I'm glad that's over with. Are you okay now?"

"I'm good," she answered brightly. "I'm still not icing yet, but I can do production and be the designated ordertaker in the meantime. See? Still wrapped."

She displayed her wrist, held steady with the brace from her night at the ER. She continued, "I'm seeing the doctor in two days to see what's next."

Jay nodded. "I hope it all goes well. We miss having your gorgeous cakes on the floor!"

Violet chuckled. "Stop it. All the cakes are gorgeous."

"Yeah, but no one's got your swirl," Jay teased, elbowing her with a laugh.

Ben stood as she and Jay shared a friendly chuckle. "I've gotta get upstairs and update the night manager before I leave. Are you all set with your stuff, Violet?"

"Yup," she replied, keeping her eyes trained on the screen as she did her best to look as casual as possible. "Thanks for letting me know about that last-minute order. I'll add it in."

From the corner of her eye, she spotted Jay watching Ben as he left. It made her wonder briefly if Jay had an ulterior motive for showing up this afternoon. Sure enough, the moment she heard the door close, Jay leaned closer.

"Vi, we've gotta chat."

She swallowed the lump that had formed in her throat as discreetly as possible. "We do?"

He paused, taking a deep breath. "There's been some talk."

Violet's eyes closed as she did her best to stomach Jay's trademark flair for the dramatic. "Who's been talking about what?"

"Some people around here have been talking about you and Ben," he replied. "They're saying you're using your relationship with him to get ahead in the company."

Some people. It took Violet less than three seconds to add up all of Jay's inquisitive conversation over the last few weeks and realize he'd been looking for something to say.

A voice in her head cursed. She knew the rules, but broke them anyway, and here Jay was actually questioning what she thought she'd hidden well. "Does anyone remember I started here before him? And that Wynne trained me personally? How can I possibly be using Ben to get ahead in the company?"

"See, that's what I thought," Jay said, sounding like a Scooby-Doo cartoon when the case was about to be cracked. "But there's something between you and Ben that I can't explain. And that's what worries me more than anything."

Her tummy churned unpleasantly. "What are you saying, Jay?"

"I'm not saying anything. What I'm asking you is

whether or not there's something going on between you and Ben."

She sighed deeply. "What makes you think there's something going on with me and Ben?"

She kept her face trained on the computer screen and perused a couple of orders, doing her best to look uninterested in the accusation placed in front of her. She could feel Jay's eyes on her like they had some sort of invisible heat beam. How long could he possibly need to watch her for a reaction?

"Well, for example, in the beginning, Wynne and I were concerned that you two would have to be separated because of all the head-bumping. And in a matter of weeks, you two are suddenly friends. Staff says the two of you stay in the office for hours, doing God knows what."

"I spend the last two and a half hours of my shift in the office doing administrative work for the store. If I tried to do it at my station, I'd never get anything done. And that's been going on since way before Ben was hired. So, what else is the staff saying?"

It was a legitimate reason, there was no denying that. She kept herself calm and even, despite the fact that the panic alarm had been going off in her head for more than twenty-four hours. Getting upset would only be an admission of guilt, and Jay would be looking for that.

"A few people have spotted you talking amongst yourselves in different areas of the store, and it apparently looks like you're hiding something."

"I'm sorry, but do you realize how ridiculous this all sounds? I interact with Ben Preston as part of my job. And yes, we bumped heads for quite a while. But, like I told Wynne, we came to an understanding. Would you rather we fight all the time?"

Jay shook his head. "Look, I understand why you'd be offended or upset. If I were being accused of—"

"It's not even that, Jay. What offends me most is that the staff is talking behind my back. Would it have hurt anyone to just come to me or Ben personally? And the fact that people seem to think I'm making my way through Wynne's Kitchen on anything other than my culinary degree and talent hurts."

"I get it, Vi. Just answer me honestly. Is there something going on between you and Ben?"

Violet took a deep breath. "No."

His lips were pressed together as he stared at the computer; Violet couldn't get a read on his reaction. Finally, he seemed to snap out of it. "Okay. If you say there's nothing going on, I believe you. But you know Wynne's stance on fraternization."

"I do," she answered, her heart growing heavy.

After a brief pause, they said in unison, "Don't do it.'"

"Exactly," Jay finished, patting her on the shoulder. "Give me a call if you need me."

And with that, he was gone. Violet slumped in her seat. She'd known this particular stretch of peace was too good to be true. She knew she had no business being upset or bitter about it; she had gotten herself into this situation. And as far as Jay confronting her, she was right not to trust him. He was a nice guy, but he was out for number one. Violet knew Wynne's Kitchen meant something to him but for different reasons. He wanted power and recognition, and she wouldn't put it past him to be the kind of guy to blow something like this out of the water for his own benefit.

Violet was closer than ever to having to make a decision—Ben or a lengthy career with the bakery? The thought of choosing hurt; she didn't want to pick one or the other. She loved being at The Rock, and that included working with the very people who were currently talking behind her back. But, unfortunately, she'd fallen head over heels for Ben. She knew she'd brought this on herself. If she'd just listened to that little voice in her head and not gotten involved, she wouldn't be on the cusp of facing some serious consequences.

∽

LATER THAT NIGHT, Ben sat with Tommy and Ethan at Crif Dogs, a gastropub with some of the greatest hot dogs known to man, located on St. Mark's Avenue in the lower part of Manhattan. Violet had promised to meet him at his place at midnight—and now, like a lovesick pup, he found himself sitting in front of a beer and one of the most insane, bacon-wrapped hot dogs he'd ever laid eyes on, counting down the minutes until he could be in a cab headed home.

Tommy gave Ethan a playful elbow. "Look at this guy. He's got a hot dog wrapped in bacon in front of him, and he still can't stop thinking about his lady."

"Easy, I'm just wondering how to start this damn thing," Ben said.

"Humph." Tommy sipped his beer. "How does it feel to be a free man?"

"I gotta say, it feels awesome," Ben replied, holding up his beer bottle in salute. "And I owe it to you and Ethan."

"Are you gonna be ring shopping for Violet now that the ink on the divorce papers is dry?" Tommy asked with a wink.

Ben laughed. "Hey now, one step at a time. I'm not rushing anything with her. I'd like this relationship to actually work out."

"So everything's good with you guys, then?" Ethan managed to get a word in edgewise.

"For sure," Ben answered. "Everything's falling into place, it's finally quiet, and we'll just focus on each other."

"Don't be so sure," Tommy remarked. "What are you going to do about the work situation?"

"What work situation? Nothing's gotten in the way of us doing our jobs, and we've kept our personal lives separate, as far as I can tell."

"He's talking about the company's fraternization policy. Or do they not have one?" Ethan asked.

Ben rolled his eyes. "Of course they have one. I just ... yeah, I ignored it." Tommy laughed. "Well, now that you've blatantly admitted to breaking policy on purpose, I have to ask—do you see this going somewhere beyond this? I know you don't want to rush, but if you had to, would you rush with her?"

Ben put his beer down, sat back, and folded his arms. "Okay, what's this actually about?"

Tommy slapped his hands on the table, pushing his chair back and standing. "It's about me, the consummate bachelor, being the voice of reason in your life ... *again*. From the way Violet talks about that bakery, she's there for the long run. It's where she wants to be right now. And your secret may be safe for now, but what about tomorrow? Or next week? It all comes out in the wash, pal. And you're putting your girl at risk."

"The only other time you were the voice of reason in my life was to tell me to either step up or break up. Do you actually want me to leave her?"

Tommy dropped his head. "If that's what you took away from what I just said, then I can't help you."

"You want to help me? Go get me another beer."

Tommy, already a little sauced, pointed an unsteady

Company Ink

finger. "Do right by this girl. She's a thousand times the woman Elena could ever even hope to be."

He turned and began to walk in the direction of the restroom. Ethan laughed as he took another swig of his beer. Ben turned to face his old friend, with whom he'd still been on shaky ground since re-entering each other's lives. "Do you have anything to say about it?"

Ethan held up his hands. "Hey, I'm still trying to prove myself here. I'll say whatever you want to hear at this point."

Ben raised an eyebrow. "That doesn't make me feel better."

"You know what I mean," Ethan insisted. "But, since you really want to know what I think, I'll tell you. Tommy's right. Violet seems to have been really good for you, and if you value her, you'll make a decision. It's the job or her, bro. I don't see it going down any other way."

Ben had been hoping for weeks that it wouldn't come to this. He had been extra careful around Violet at work, especially since he had begun quietly coaching her as Wynne requested. However, he was skeptical—as busy as the store was on a normal basis, there was no way anyone in the company was paying that much attention.

"Bah," Ben huffed, reaching for his beer. "Can't we just have a happy medium? Where we get to enjoy each other both in our personal and professional lives?"

"In a perfect world, I guess. But you and I both know that world doesn't exist."

∼

BY A QUARTER TO MIDNIGHT, Ben was happily headed uptown to his condo, where he knew Violet was waiting for him. He popped an Altoid in his mouth as he stared out the cab window, feeling a little guilty that he'd be arriving home with the smell of hot dog and a six-pack on his breath. His head swam as they made their way up the West Side Highway and, try as he might to enjoy the buzz, he couldn't help but go back to what Tommy said. Deep down, Ben knew he couldn't continue to play roulette with their careers.

There wasn't a doubt in his mind about his relationship with Violet—he wouldn't be ring shopping tomorrow or next week, but he knew it was coming. Violet was a woman to love and a woman to marry. She not only made life and love effortless, but she made it worth fighting for, as well. He could easily envision a life with her, and if the two of them working together would eventually become a problem, then it was one he needed to solve. He'd discuss it with her tonight. They could look at everything objectively, talk about it, and go from there. All thoughts of rational discussion disappeared, however, when he opened the door to his condo and found a trail of rose petals leading to the bathroom. The door was open, candlelight flickered from inside, and the sound of the shower mingled with Violet's soft melodic voice as she hummed an unknown tune.

Deciding that no words would be necessary for the moment, he kicked off his shoes at the door. He then headed down the hall, peeling off his clothing layer by layer until he stood before the bathroom, stark naked. He could see Violet's silhouette through the shower curtain as she stood under the water stream, soaking her hair and running her hands over her flat tummy and rounded hips. He licked his lips briefly, and her soft singing stopped.

"Welcome home," she murmured, the smile on her face apparent though he couldn't see her.

"What a welcome home it is."

"Do I have to ask you to come in, Ben?"

He reached for the shower curtain, slowly tugging it back. "No, but I plan on making you beg later."

Violet giggled as he stepped in. "We'll see about that."

Her back arched as he lifted her chin with one crooked finger and leaned in for a kiss. She sighed against his mouth, pressing her body into his and submitting to his touch immediately. Ben cupped the back of her head as he deepened their kiss. There would be time for talking later.

∼

BEN SAT up in bed early the next morning, taking care not to wake the sleeping sex kitten next to him. He smiled, thinking with a silent chuckle that Violet might kill him before either of them had to worry about the folks at Wynne's finding out about them. He stepped out of the bedroom, closing the door behind him gently as he carried an armful of clothes to the bathroom. They were both off today; he had a couple of appointments to keep this morning, but there was no reason to disturb Violet. He'd even bring back something tasty for breakfast, for the purpose of refueling, of course. He imagined spending the rest of the day making love to the curvaceous goddess sleeping in his bed. He crept out of the condo at about seven, planning on being back as fast as he feasibly could.

Ben met with his accountant and financial advisor first, dropping off his proof of the divorce settlement so that there would be no confusion where alimony was concerned. He ended up having coffee with them and discussing his investment portfolio, which, he was surprised to learn, was doing better than anticipated. Afterwards, he bumped into an old friend from the restaurant industry, and they had coffee at a small table in Grand Central Station, where the friend, who happened to be a regional manager for 5 Napkin Restaurants. So Ben was running a couple of hours behind on his errands, but he walked through Midtown with a genuine smile on his face. Life was, suffice it to say, close to perfect. Something caught Ben's eye as he made his way down Lexington Avenue; he stopped in front of a jewelry store to stare at a bevy of opulent engagement rings.

He leaned in, perusing the selection. Most of the rings were priced higher than what his condo cost. But Violet was worth every penny, and he'd gladly risk going broke to make her happy. He straightened with a start when someone cleared their throat behind him.

"Sorry, I didn't mean to get in the … "

Elena stood before him, arms folded as she tapped her red Manolo heel impatiently.

"Is this what you're doing already? Do you think that girl's actually going to marry you?"

Ben tilted his head back, letting out a sigh. "Where did you come from? Are you following me again?"

"Maybe I am, but only because I've got something that can't wait."

"Is it cancer?"

Elena clucked her tongue at him. "Now, now, don't be bitter. You stopped me from getting what I want, isn't that enough?"

"Jesus, Elena," he replied, pinching the bridge of his nose with his thumb and forefinger. "I can't believe I actually married you."

"I can't believe I married you, either, Ben. And I can't believe that, after you managed to take away everything that was rightfully mine, I still managed to get such an amazing present."

"Okay, fine. What are we talking about?"

Elena smiled, batting her false eyelashes at him. "Well,

my parents came up from Virginia over the weekend. And of course, they wanted to do the tourist thing. So I took them all over the city, and they mentioned that the city never seemed this interesting when you were around, and I said—"

"The point, Elena."

"Right, the point. We headed over to Rockefeller Center and took pictures of everything. The skating rink, the statues, and the sign above the entrance to CBS Studios—we got it all. Then they wanted to go see some world-famous bakery called Wynne's Kitchen. You've heard of it, haven't you?"

Ben held his breath. "I have. Go on."

"Well, we headed over there and looked in the window to see what the crowd was like," she continued, taking a couple of menacing steps toward him. "When, lo and behold, we spotted a familiar face."

Ben said nothing.

"I had no idea you were still in the food industry, hon." Elena's voice was ominous. "Well, up until yesterday, I thought I would be paying for your shopping sprees and

spa days," he retorted. "I had to find a job somewhere, didn't I?"

Elena gave him a confident grin. "Be that as it may, we ended up not going in because, believe it or not, my parents decided they couldn't possibly stomach a cupcake while having to look at you."

"I'm sure the scathing disappointment in their only child was more than enough for them to bear."

"Cute. I suggested we stick around for a few minutes to see if you would leave. I really did want them to have some of the delicious treats on display, so we stayed. And let me tell you, I found something much more delicious than any cupcake.

"I'm standing in front of the window, watching a girl ice a red velvet cake. She's doing an amazing job, when her supervisor approaches with a clipboard to talk to her.

And here's where it gets interesting—I recognized the supervisor!"

Ben froze—he'd been caught. He hadn't been as worried about Wynne making the connection as he'd been about Elena. He'd thought he might have been in the clear, but as he saw the vindictive look in his ex-wife's eyes, he knew he'd been living in a fool's paradise.

Chapter Thirteen

Of all the things in the world she could have said, this truly wasn't what he expected. He kept his mouth set in a firm line, refusing to reveal to Elena that she'd just pulled a playable card.

"Oh, yeah," she said. "Your girl is working in the same store. I recognized her almost immediately! You know, most reputable companies have strict anti-fraternization policies, don't they?"

Anger bubbled just beneath the surface, and he felt himself getting ready to say something stupid. But, oddly enough, he couldn't shake snippets of his conversation with Ethan, and it made him want to appeal to her instead. There had to be some decency in there.

"Elena, listen—"

"I think Wynne herself would probably be grateful for a call that might alert her to any unsavory activity occurring in her company," she said, tilting her head to one side. "Tsk, tsk, Benji. You should be ashamed of yourself."

He held up a hand to stop her from talking. "Elena, please. Just hear me out. I couldn't figure out what I did wrong or what would make you decide to be so ... awful. I mean, I gave you everything you asked for—money, clothes, and even space, against my better judgment. And then I thought about what you said to me when you showed up at the condo. You said I tried to make you into something you weren't."

He had her attention. Her expression was fixed into one of confusion. "Ben, what are you—"

"You said that I beat you into submission—but that wasn't it. I bought you into submission. I threw money at all of our problems. I never let you know that I was there for you. So in a way, you're right—I tried to make you something you weren't."

Confusion gave way to pain as tears filled her eyes. She turned away from him. "Stop it, Ben."

He hadn't heard her sound anything other than disdainful in months, so he continued.

"No, Elena. I owe you an apology. I'm sorry for making you feel like you had to be anything other than yourself."

He heard Elena sniff. She reached up and wiped her eyes. "I hate you."

"I know," he answered. "I don't think I can do anything about that. But I hope you can move on and find whatever it is you're looking for."

She drew in a deep breath and turned around, dabbing tears from under her eyes with one slender finger. "Well, Ben, I'll tell you what I'm not looking for—your apologies or your sympathy. Do you think that blowing smoke up my ass is going to distract me from keeping that promise I made to you? I guess we'll just have to see what Wynne's opinion is on all of this."

Ben shook his head as he watched her pull her cell phone out and start swiping through it. She was shaken, he could tell. But he wasn't apologizing for any other reason than that he got it. He knew where he'd gone wrong. And while it didn't excuse her adultery and less-than-savory behavior up until this point, he had hoped the validation would help. But if she was still bent on carrying out her agenda, then he would have to beat her to the punch.

"I'm really not looking to charm you into backing off. I just wanted you to know—"

"Save it, honey. The world is going to know how disgusting you are, starting with Wynne's Kitchen."

He straightened, going from panic mode to anger to calm resignation in a matter of seconds. Ben briefly held his hands up in defeat before letting his arms drop to his sides.

"You know what? You win. Do what you've gotta do." He took long strides away from her, stopping at the curb to hail a cab.

"I mean it, Ben! It's ringing!"

He didn't give her a second glance. "Congratulations."

Thankfully, a cab screeched to a stop in front of him. He climbed in, trying to ignore Elena's demands for attention as she spoke loudly on the phone to whom he assumed was the receptionist in Wynne's corporate office.

He took a deep breath and told the cab driver, "Sixty-Eighth and Freedom Place, please."

⁂

VIOLET WOKE up at around nine, the sun leaking in through the small openings in Ben's blinds. He was gone, of course; she knew he had a couple of errands to run today. She turned over and buried her face in his pillow, inhaling deeply. His intoxicating scent filled her nostrils, and she grabbed the pillow with a smile, as if it were a teddy bear. She rolled over with a happy groan, blissful despite the fact that the chickens were coming home to roost.

Violet let her legs hang over the side of the bed as she allowed herself one glorious stretch before venturing out into the rest of the apartment. She began her morning routine, wondering what time Ben would be home. It occurred to her as she was midway through making a pot of coffee that she wouldn't mind waking up next to him on a regular basis or having a pot of coffee ready for him upon his return. The thought made her smile.

About an hour later, she was happily enjoying a second cup of coffee along with a small stack of cinnamon toast at the dinette in the kitchen, where she was reading *The New York Times* which had been left at the door moments before. Her phone buzzed loudly from the bedroom. She jogged over to check it, assuming it would be Ben. She saw Wynne's name on the screen.

So much for blissful ignorance.

She cleared her throat and put on her best happy voice. "Good morning, Wynne!"

"Good morning, sweetie. How's the wrist?"

"Feeling good," she replied. "But I don't see the doctor until tomorrow morning."

"That sounds hopeful," Wynne commented pleasantly. "And you'll be at work after?"

"Yes, ma'am. Is everything okay?"

Wynne took an audible breath before finally saying, "I really wanted to wait until tomorrow to discuss this with you, but I can't pretend I'm not seriously concerned about what I'm hearing."

Here we go. Violet sighed. "Is this about what Jay and I discussed yesterday?"

Company Ink

"You hit the nail on the head. Jay's telling me that you're denying any involvement with Ben Preston?"

Tears sprang to Violet's eyes. She squeezed her eyes shut, angry at herself for the lie she was about to tell a second time in as many days. "I'm denying it."

There was a long stretch of silence on the other end. Every second that passed felt like a stab in the chest. Finally, Wynne asked, "Are you telling me the truth, Vi?"

"Yes," she answered quickly, calmly. She stared at the damp towel—Ben's towel—hanging on the door hook as she paced into the bathroom and sat on the tub. "There's nothing going on with me and Ben."

"Violet, I don't know what else to say. I take my policies seriously. I've heard from many of the staff and others that the two of you have been together for weeks now. It's simply unacceptable, and I can't worry about things like this while I'm trying to run a company. Do you understand what I'm saying?"

Violet tugged at her curls, trying to keep from bursting into tears. It was like Wynne was seeing her through the phone, on Ben's tub in Ben's condo—wearing Ben's boxers.

"I do."

"You know I love having you here. There isn't anything I wouldn't do to make your growth with us comfortable. But I can't budge on this. And if I were to find out that you were lying to me ... Well, Vi, that's just a betrayal of the worst kind."

"I get it."

"Then tell me the truth. Are they wrong? Is there really nothing between you and Ben?"

Violet wrapped an arm around her middle to try to halt the pangs of nausea. "There's nothing going on."

Wynne sighed. "Okay, Violet. I believe you. I just

needed to talk to you now, to put my mind at ease. And I'm sorry to put so much stress on you; I know you work exceptionally hard every minute you're in the store."

"Thanks."

"We'll talk more when you're in, okay? Try and enjoy the rest of your day off. We'll see you tomorrow."

"Okay, thanks."

Violet ended the call with a weary goodbye; she placed the phone on the edge of the sink and sat with her head in her hands for what felt like hours. She'd officially lied to her mentor. Wynne had become such an important part of her development as a baker and future entrepreneur, she may as well have lied to her own grandmother. Gran might have been rolling over in her grave right now, appalled at Violet's behavior. *Lying to the woman who took a chance on you to save your ass and continuing to sleep with your manager.*

Violet dropped to her knees in front of the toilet and threw up.

∼

BEN ARRIVED home at around one o' clock, two hours later than he had planned. He carried with him a bag of bagels and containers of various spreads for them to try. He smelled coffee in the air and smiled at the thought that he and Violet were so on the same wavelength.

"Vi?"

No answer. He walked into the kitchen and placed the bag of goodies on the dinette table. He then poured himself a cup of coffee before looking for Violet in the bedroom. There she was, huddled under a pile of blankets.

Smiling, he stared at the lump while taking a sip of his

Company Ink

coffee. One of her legs stuck out from beneath the blanket as she lay completely still. "Good morning, sunshine."

At the sound of his voice, she moved and pulled her leg under the blanket so that she disappeared completely. He heard her gasp and sniffle and put his cup down in concern, taking a seat beside her immediately.

"Vi, are you crying?"

She sniffled again, her voice muffled. "No."

Ben grabbed a handful of blanket and pulled it aside. Sure enough, Violet lay there with her hair in a messy bun and her eyes red and swollen.

"What happened, sweetheart?"

Violet sighed. "I have something to tell you."

"Okay." He rubbed her back consolingly. "It must be something important, since you're lying here sobbing like someone died."

Violet sucked her teeth. "Ben, could you not?"

"I'm just trying to lighten the mood. Tell me what's happened between the time I left this morning and right now that's got you so upset."

"Yesterday, after you left the office, Jay and I had a talk."

He already knew what it was about. "Really, about what?"

"The staff's been talking about us. They started telling Jay that it looks like you and I have something going on."

"Hmm," he remarked. "Pretty astute, aren't they?"

She turned onto her back and stared at him in disbelief. "Seriously?"

"I'm sorry, go on."

"He asked if you and I were seeing each other," she continued, putting one arm over her eyes, "and I said no."

"Okay." He nodded. "Good answer. Did he leave it at that?"

"Well, I thought that was it. He seemed to believe me. And after last night ... well, I kind of forgot about it."

Ben smiled, flattening his hand on her bare belly. "Yeah, last night was fun."

Violet finally grinned. "Like I said, I forgot about it."

Ben bent forward and placed a soft kiss where his hand had been. He wasn't worried anymore; he just wished he could explain it to her. "Tell me more, Vi. I mean, if you can."

Violet struggled to sit up. "Ben, come on!"

He climbed onto the bed and crawled on top of her body. His hands teased the soft flesh of her waist as he sampled her neck with the tip of his tongue. "What? I'm listening."

"Wynne called this morning! She asked me what was going on, and I lied. I don't know what to do at this point. The last thing I wanted was to lie to her!"

Ben stretched his body over hers, gently coaxing her legs apart to settle his weight on top of her.

"I don't think you get what's going on right now," Violet gasped, trying to lock eyes with him.

"Sweetheart, I know exactly what's going on," he murmured, planting a kiss on her chin before moving down to nibble on her collarbone.

"You're sure being nonchalant about all of this."

He pressed his pelvis against hers; her eyes widened slightly. His mouth closed over hers. He'd already made a huge decision and taken steps to see it through. But he knew— and adored—the built-in heroine switch that existed in Violet's body, and if he divulged what he'd done, she'd never let him go through with it. So he set about on a new mission—to distract his girlfriend from the situation at hand.

"I would just rather spend my time enjoying my girlfriend and our incredible"—he paused to nip at the hollow of her throat—"*incredible* sexual chemistry than worry about what people are saying about us."

Despite the fact that she wanted him inside her more than she wanted to be concerned, she persisted. "But what about—"

"Sweetheart," Ben interrupted, his voice husky and demanding, "we'll work it out. Don't worry about it, not right now."

She looked up at him imploringly, as if she were asking him to make it all go away.

"Let me handle it," he murmured. "Okay?"

He leaned down to kiss her again, determined to make her forget about the mounting pressure their secret relationship had begun to apply on their lives, at least for one night.

∽

VIOLET COULDN'T EVEN REJOICE over the doctor's news that her wrist had healed well. She should have been happy, but she really felt like she was being sent to her death. She knew she'd crumble the moment she saw Wynne and there would be no way she could leave The Rock at the end of her shift still gainfully employed.

She dragged her feet as she wove her way through the huge crowd of tourists and other dessert-seekers. She ignored the hellos from staff members that followed her down to the basement. She was angry with them for kicking up dirt that had been just fine where it was. Then she guiltily apologized to them in her head, knowing she'd brought this entire situation on herself. She took a deep breath before stepping into the office.

She was surprised to find Jay and Wynne sitting there,

with Wynne occupying Ben's desk. They were huddled around Ben's computer, looking through pages of reports and deposit slips. They didn't seem to notice her arrival; Violet raised a quizzical eyebrow as she watched them interact.

"Everything's in order," Jay said.

"Shame," Wynne answered with a shake of her head. "It could've worked out."

Deciding she didn't want to hear more, Violet let the door close loudly behind her.

Both Wynne and Jay spun around, startled, as she walked over to her desk.

Wynne was the first to speak. "Oh, Violet! How was the doctor visit?"

"It went well," she replied, holding up her wrist. "Soft brace and I can resume my normal activities. Gradually, of course."

Wynne smiled. "That is great news."

"Congrats, Vi," Jay added with a supportive grin.

"Thanks," she replied, placing her backpack under her desk and taking a seat. "So, what have I missed?"

Jay and Wynne looked at each other, as if silently deciding who should speak first. It was Wynne, of course.

"Actually, you missed something huge this morning. Ben Preston no longer works here."

Violet could've been knocked over with a feather. She struggled to hide the fact that her stomach had just dropped into her feet. "Wow, really? What happened?"

"Well, I got here and he let me know immediately that he'd experienced a family tragedy last night," Jay explained, clearly still stunned. "He said it would be taking him out of the state for quite a few weeks, and he didn't think it was fair to leave us hanging for so long. So he resigned."

Company Ink

Violet's jaw dropped. "Wow. Talk about a bombshell!"

Wynne watched her carefully. Violet knew she was doing a great job of concealing the gamut of emotions she was currently going through if Wynne couldn't get a read on her. But on the inside, she was having a conniption. She was fighting every urge to jump to her feet, run upstairs, and call him to find out why he'd up and left the company without so much as a word to her.

"It was definitely a bombshell," Wynne agreed. "Jay's going to be acting manager until we hire someone new. I'm sorry to have to do this to you, but we're gonna need you to step up and help pick up some of the slack while we select a new manager."

Violet nodded. "Sure. Not a problem."

"And can we count on you to help with training again?"

"Absolutely," Violet replied, feeling like her insides were on fire.

"I hope it's okay if I start back with icing tomorrow," she added as casually as possible. "Let today's icer finish her week out; it'll give my wrist one more day of rest. Maybe I'll do some cupcakes later to test the waters."

"That sounds good," Wynne replied from behind her. "And, uh, needless to say, the conversation we were supposed to continue today is a little redundant at this point, agreed?"

Violet closed her eyes briefly, fighting the urge to let out a sigh of relief. "Agreed."

She knew the family tragedy thing was a lie, but what about his decision to quit? Surely they could have thought of a different solution! She managed to keep her cool for the first half of her day, even when all she wanted to do was run upstairs and call Ben. Her phone remained silent throughout the first part of her shift; no signal in the basement meant no text messages, no word from Ben on why he'd done it without so much as a word to her. By the time her break time rolled around, she thought she was going to lose it.

She made it upstairs and out of the store, walking directly past the row of street vendors along Sixth Avenue as she waited for her phone to pick up signal again. When it finally did, her phone didn't make a sound. Growing angry, she sent Ben a text message and waited. When he didn't answer within his customary five minutes, her heart picked up speed. She dialed his number—no answer. In fact, it went straight to voicemail. His phone was off? *What the hell is going on?*

Violet spent the remainder of her shift pissed that she had to hold everything in until it was time to go home. Her fingers flew over the keyboard as she accepted a Seamless order for the next morning.

"Are you okay, Vi?"

Violet quickly plastered a smile on her face. "I'm fine, Wynne. Just giving my wrist a workout; I wanna make sure I'm up for some icing tomorrow."

Wynne sat down next to her. "Is that all?"

Violet glanced at her mentor with a more relaxed smile, determined to keep everything under wraps. "That's all. I'm in a little pain though, truth be told."

Wynne gave her a sympathetic expression. "You should really take it easy. Why don't you head home and put some ice on that thing?"

"Are you sure? I don't want to leave the store short-staffed."

"Go home." Wynne sounded like a mother now. "Ice that wrist and come back in the morning ready to resume your usual post at the icer's station."

Violet heaved a sigh, feigning disappointment when she

was already picturing hailing a cab and hightailing it to Riverside Boulevard. "All right, I guess I'll do that."

"I'm interested in seeing your speed after all of this."

Violet chuckled. "If my speed suffered at all, I'm hiring a hit man to go after my ex."

Wynne laughed, rubbing Violet's shoulder. "You'll get it back, I'm sure of it."

Violet grabbed her bag with her good hand and tossed it over her shoulder with a grin. "I hope you're right."

"I know I am." Wynne smiled. "Like I know I'm right about you. Everything's going to be fine, you'll see."

Violet made her way out of the store knowing that, because of Ben's sacrifice, she'd managed to keep her job. But that didn't relieve him of any of the nervous anger she was about to unleash on him ...

∽

SHE BURST into Ben's apartment less than forty-five minutes later, a bag in her hand. The smell of spaghetti sauce filled the house; he was cooking dinner like nothing had happened! Dropping the plastic bag and her knapsack on the couch, she headed straight for the kitchen, where Ben was standing over a pot and stirring with a contented smile on his face.

"Hey, sweetheart."

Violet raised an eyebrow. "That's what you have to say?"

"Did you want a serenade?"

She shifted her weight to one side, fighting a smile. "Damn it, Ben."

He placed his wooden spoon on the stove and approached her. Winding his arms around her waist, he smiled playfully. "What?"

Violet put her hands on his chest, trying halfheartedly to push him away. "A family tragedy?"

Grinning proudly, he replied, "I told you I'd handle it."

"But, Ben—quitting? Why didn't you tell me?"

"Because you wouldn't have let me."

"You're damn right I wouldn't have let you! You need your job as much as I need mine."

"Except that your job is your career. I couldn't care less about baking in general. I can have a new job in a week."

Violet sighed. "Are you sure?"

He nodded. "I'm sure. Look, I'm going to tell you something, but I don't want you to get upset. I saw Elena yesterday."

She blinked. "I definitely didn't expect that. What happened?"

"Well, she found out by way of her touristy parents that you and I were working in the same company. And she threatened to go to Wynne."

"Are you kidding me? Is that why Wynne called me? If I ever—"

"I don't know if she actually called, Vi," Ben interrupted, raising his voice just enough to stop her rant. "I walked away from her. But between that and the conversation I had with Tommy and Ethan, I realized—"

"What?" Violet asked, stunned. "When were you going to tell me—"

With a smile, Ben placed a finger on her lips, effectively silencing her. "Let me finish. Between my conversation with the guys and Elena's persistent nonsense, I realized that you and I were setting ourselves up for implosion if we kept sneaking around like this."

Violet nodded. "I did, too."

"See, then you understand," he continued. "I was in a

position to make a choice, to end this entire mess with one decision. So I did."

"But, Ben—"

"No buts. The choice was easy for me. It's you. It always has been."

Violet took a minute to absorb what he'd done for her. She wouldn't have to face any humiliation or any more questioning. She could simply have both things she wanted desperately: her burgeoning career and the man she loved.

"Well, now I feel like a jerk," she said. "I was completely at a loss for what to do. I didn't want to quit, but I didn't want to lose you."

Ben smiled. "Stop, Vi. I wouldn't have expected you to sacrifice your career to be with me. For me, Wynne's was just a bakery. I could be managing a steakhouse in a week for all I care. It's just how I earn my money."

She hugged him as hard as her trembling arms would allow. "Thank you."

Ben kissed the top of her head. "Now do me favor. Make your way up the ranks at Wynne's, then leave and open up the quintessential bakery that will put her out of business."

Violet laughed into his chest. "That's awful!"

"Too soft to dethrone your mentor?"

"I guess so," she giggled, looking up at him. "But that's why you love me."

Ben chuckled, caressing her jawline with one finger. "That's not the only reason."

Violet stood on her tiptoes and wrapped her arms around his neck as he gently pressed his forehead against her shoulder. "You still smell like cupcakes."

About the Author

Samantha Anne is a writer, bassist, baker, and proud Hufflepuff. Currently based in Texas, she loves where she is and what her new surroundings have done for her, but she will never forget that The Bronx, New York is the home that raised her. When she's not writing or encouraging others to write, she is painting or crocheting while flanked by her cats Alfie and Claire, who love watching Netflix movies and sleeping while she works. To know Samantha is to learn to expect anything from her, whether it's a new full length novel, a screenplay, a fun recipe series on her blog, a punk album, or a solo ukulele EP.

Learn more about Samantha and her various projects by visiting **www.samantha-anne.net**

Made in United States
Orlando, FL
12 May 2023